For Shirley -
my friend whom
I miss. Enjoy!
Judy
4/2023

Sterling Script

A Local Author Collection
2022

Walper Publishing
Sterling Heights, Michigan

Editors
Tuesday Morning Writers
Rena Davis, Katy Hojnacki,
Terry Hojnacki, Teresa Moy, and Rebecca Eve Schweitzer

Editor-in-Chief
Terry Hojnacki

Cover Art & Design
Katy Hojnacki

ISBN: 978-1-949224-08-5
Volume Five of the Local Author Collection

The selections printed in this collection reflect the authors'
original work as submitted to the
Local Author Collection.

First Edition
1 2 3 4 5 6 7 8 9 10

Many thanks
to the authors and editors
in our vibrant writing community
for making this project possible—

Happy Writing

Table of Contents

Dear Reader,

Each year comes with its own unique challenges. This one did not disappoint. I'm proud to say we conquered every glitch and put together the fifth edition of Sterling Script: A Local Author Collection.

My team of editors, who volunteer their time and talent for this project, have my sincere thanks and gratitude. Together, our mission remains strong. We strive to encourage our local writers by publishing their short stories, poetry, and creative non-fiction works.

As Nathaniel Hawthorne said, "Good reading is damn hard writing." Our authors have put in the hard work writing.

Happy Reading,
Terry

A.J. Douglas

A.J. Douglas is a lover of all things fantasy and comedy, especially when they're combined. She loves to write high fantasy elements like magic, far off places, and dragons blended with modern-esque themes.

She began writing at a young age, starting with fanfiction. Most of her early work still lurks within the bowels of the internet. She also dreamed up and wrote her first full novel while pretending to pay attention during high school Spanish class.

A.J. resides in Oakland County with her husband and two rambunctious little boys. She is a member of the Sterling Heights Creative Writers' Workshop, sometimes drops in at local author cons/events, and can also be followed on twitter @authorajdouglas.

A Little Teleportation Is a Dangerous Thing

A.J. Douglas

Air whooshed past Delinda as she clung to her father's back. The forest green dragon's ruby-colored wings beat in a steady rhythm, propelling them over the city streets. Sounds of traffic echoed off the buildings they soared between.

They leaned into a left turn on to the road leading to the banquet hall. The skirt of her lavender dress rippled around her legs. She hoped that the edges of it hadn't started to fray.

"Daaaad!" Delinda whined, feeling strands from her updo coming free. "I thought I asked you to take those turns slower! It's messing up my hair!" Her stylist used almost an entire bottle of magi-hold hairspray to get it to stay in place.

"Sorry, sweetheart," he called from the front of the saddle. "We can only go so slow without risking losing altitude."

She rolled her eyes at his excuse. He still acted like she'd never flown a dragon before. Whipping around turns was fun and all, but was now the time for that?

The grand marble-pillared banquet hall hosting her end-of-year senior class formal came into view. Brightly lit floor-to-ceiling windows spanned across its front. Cars and limousines lined the driveway, stretching out into the road as her classmates arrived. She wondered if her boyfriend, Tamil, was in one of those limos. He and a bunch of others split the cost of one. She wanted to go with them as well, but her dad insisted that he take his only daughter to her last school dance. She just didn't expect him to make a show of it, traveling by dragon. But that's the life of a dragon trainer's

3

daughter for you.

They slowed on their final approach, coming to a glide as her father circled the parking lot for an appropriate place to set the creature down. It began to draw the attention from the crowds of students and parents. Her family's business wasn't unknown to the rest of the community. But it also wasn't every day they swooped in on the backs of the giant fire-breathing beasts, either.

"Descendere!" her father ordered, with a tug on the reins.

Their mount obliged, raising her wings into a wide V-formation and landing gracefully on an empty section of pavement to the side of the building. She folded her wings and squatted, allowing her passengers to dismount.

Delinda's father was first to slide from the saddle, turning to offer his daughter a hand.

A group of people started to approach them. This was the part she always hated. She bowed her head and tucked back lose strands of red hair in an attempt to hide her embarrassment. "Dad, I know how to get down," Delinda grumbled.

"I know you do, sweetie. But I thought you could use a hand in that dress and heels."

She huffed and accepted. "Fine. Thanks, Dad." Once her feet were on the ground, she muttered a quick goodbye and tried to hurry away from the curious onlookers, only for her father to call her back.

"Aren't you forgetting something?" He gave her an expectant look.

"What?" She hiked her silver sequined purse higher on her shoulder, wanting nothing more than to escape the gawkers, fix her hair, and find Tam and the rest of their friends.

"A hug for your old man, maybe."

"Ugh…" she groaned, her matching silver pumps clacking on the pavement as she hurriedly stomped back to him for a quick side hug.

"Stay safe. Have fun. Say 'hi' to Tam for us. Are you going

4

to need a ride home?"

"I'm going back to Hazel's house for the night, remember? She's having us girls over for a scary movie marathon."

"Ah, right." Her dad released her. "See you tomorrow. Be sure to at least text your mom an update or two."

Delinda left so her father could engage in his second favorite part about raising dragons: showing them off. He'd probably be there for at least another hour.

Jeweled chandeliers hung from the ceilings of the hall, enchanted with a spell that showered gold flecks halfway to the ground before disappearing. Dozens of round tables draped with white cloths filled the room. A D.J. in the corner of the dance floor played jazzy instrumentals while students continued to arrive in droves.

Stepping away from the stream of arrivals pouring through the doors, Delinda texted Tam to see if he was here and had a table yet.

He didn't even bother to respond. Just shouted her name across the room, making almost everyone look in her direction, and waved her down.

She *tsked* and rolled her eyes, starting toward a table close to the dance floor. He was with her bestie Hazel and some members of the Teen Magic-Casters Club.

"You could've messaged me instead of yelling." She set her purse on the table in front of a chair next to his.

Tam shrugged. "Eh, it was easier than typing it out." He smiled at the sight of her. "Don't you look beautiful?" He cleaned up well himself, trading in his usual gamer-nerd shirt and cargo pants for a suit that complimented his tan complexion and dark hair. Tam reached for his Beasty Bards water bottle and took a sip. His eyes bulged as he nearly spit it out. He forced himself to swallow, rather than spray his girlfriend. "Ugh! What's up with my water? Did the bottle not get cleaned right?" He looked inside, swirling the liquid around.

5

"What's wrong?" Delinda asked.

He set the bottle down, trading it for a napkin. "I dunno. It tasted really off. Bitter or something. I should dump it before I drink more on accident."

"If you're gonna go do that, I'm gonna fix up my hair. Dad was being a cowboy with the dragon again."

"Oh! I'll come with you!" Hazel broke off from the conversation she was having with one of her club members.

Delinda grabbed her purse, and the two headed across the hall to the women's room. "So, how was the limo?" she asked while they navigated through the crowd. "I'm so jealous you got to ride in one."

"I didn't." Hazel's expression soured. "Got pulled into work last minute. Ended up driving myself."

"That sucks." She pushed the swinging door to the restroom open. "Sorry you had to miss it."

The pair approached the mirror and squeezed in for a sliver of space amongst the row of other girls. The mixed scents of perfume and hair products hung like a thick cloud in the air. Delinda held her breath, resisting the urge to sneeze from her triggered allergies, as she tucked extra bobby pins into her updo.

By the time the girls returned to their table, Tamil still hadn't. His water bottle was in front of his seat, though.

Delinda sat and pointed to the bottle. "Did Tam come back and then leave again?" she asked another student at the table.

The boy shook his head. "No. Haven't seen him. Edric left that there a minute ago. Come to think of it, he was looking for Tam as well."

While unfolding her napkin on her lap, Delinda's eyes scanned around the room. There was no sign of him anywhere. Or Edric, one of their classmates who shared the limo ride.

Hazel took her seat next to Delinda. "Wait, what's going on?"

"Tam hasn't come back yet." Delinda reached for her purse, pulled open the clasp, and removed her phone. She noticed it was set to silent and already had missed calls from him. "Now why is he..." Delinda wondered aloud as she clicked to return his most recent one, hoping something wasn't wrong.

"Finally! Lind, where have you been?" Tam's panicked voiced answered before the first ring finished.

"I could ask you the same! Wait, are you outside?" She heard wind and the rush of evening traffic on his end. "What are you doing out there?"

"That's what *I* wanna know! I was looking for a water fountain to dump the bottle when I blinked and all of a sudden, I'm standing in some creepy alley! So, I left to see where I was, and I'm near the Smoothie Sorcerer."

Delinda pressed her fingers into her temple. "The Smoothie Sorcerer? That's all the way by the mall! How'd you get there?"

"*The mall?*" Hazel mouthed.

Delinda waved her off before plugging her ear to block out the noise from the room.

"No idea," he said. "But I was just thinking about a spellbound strawberry fro-lixor."

"Really, Tam?" Delinda scoffed, tossing her hand in the air. "We're about to have a fancy buffet dinner with a full mocktail bar, and you're thinking about fro-lixors?"

"You know those are my favorite, Lind." An electronic door chime dinged as he spoke.

"D-did you just go *in?*"

"Yeah, what do you expect me to do, stand around on the side of the road in my suit? If I'm here, I'm getting one while we figure this out."

Delinda sighed. "Listen, my dad might still be here with the dragon. I'll see if he can go get you. Enjoy your drink."

"You're the best!"

She groaned, clicking *end call,* and faced Hazel. "Somehow,

7

he… teleported or something to the smoothie place by the mall."

"Teleported?" Hazel raised her brow. "You don't think someone spiked his water or hexed him, do you?"

She made a high-pitched hum and shrugged. "I'll be right back. I'm gonna go see if my dad is still here." Delinda stood and hurried out the front door. Her father was nowhere to be seen, but there was still a group of curious onlookers gathered in the parking lot, watching something up above. "Don't tell me…" She shifted her eyes skyward as well.

In the air, her dad and the dragon performed a loop-dee-loop, earning an uproarious applause from the crowd.

"Really?" She stopped just short of rubbing a hand across her face, remembering her copious amounts of eye makeup. Flexing her fingers, she lowered her arm and turned to head back inside. If he was busy with his tricks, there was no way she'd get his attention.

Her phone started ringing. The selfie of her and Tam at the summer concert came up on the screen. Delinda clicked *accept*. "Hello—"

"I'm a criminal!" Tamil cried on the other end.

She stopped walking. Her heart thudded in her chest upon hearing his distress. "Why? What's wrong?"

Tam hurriedly began to explain. "I was at the register ready to pay for my drink, but before I could give the cashier my money, I teleported away! I don't know what happened! Now I'm probably banned from Smoothie Sorcerer for life! They'll think I'm a thief!"

How was any of this happening? "Listen, just calm down. I'll find a way to come get you, we'll go back to Smoothie Sorcerer, explain what happened, and pay."

"I thought your dad was coming?"

She glanced over her shoulder at the people in the parking lot cheering him on. "Ummm… he won't be. Hang on a little longer, and I'll figure it out. Do you know where you are?"

"I dunno… Some roof."

"You're on a roof?"

"Yeah. I think it's also by the mall. But man, the smell of fries is making me hungry! I was just thinking I could go for some... wait!" He gasped. "I know where I am! It's Fry Friar!"

Delinda walked at a hurried pace through the banquet hall, dodging the frenzy of activity as the last of the arriving students claimed their tables. "Okay... I'll see if Hazel will loan me her car. In the meantime, see if there's a ladder or some way to get down from there."

"Got it!"

She hung up. Appetizing aromas of meats, pasta and vegetables coming from the kitchen doors made her stomach rumble. Delinda glanced at the time on her phone. Dinner was set to begin soon. Hopefully, Hazel would be open to helping her, and she wouldn't miss the whole meal.

At their table, her friend stood in front of Edric with folded arms and a scowl. The elven teen had a guilty look on his face, running his fingers through his long black hair.

"There you are!" Hazel greeted Delinda as she neared.

"What's going on?"

Hazel waved her hand at Edric. "Go on, tell her what happened!"

"Look, it was supposed to be a harmless prank!" He gave Delinda a pleading look.

Delinda's fists snapped to her waist. "What. Did. You. Do?" Hearing herself say it like that gave her pause for a moment, realizing how much she sounded like her mom just then.

Edric's shoulders slumped as he breathed a loud sigh. "I was gonna do the ol' teleportation-potion-in-the-punchbowl trick." His hands cobbled around his words as he spoke, before falling limp at his sides. "The concentration was only supposed to have people zapping around the ballroom for a little while. It was gonna be funny! But it looks like my water bottle and Tam's got mixed up on the limo ride and he...

9

drank a full, undiluted dose."

Stunned, Delinda stood with her jaw hung open, loss for words.

"My thoughts exactly," Hazel cut in. "Now Tam's going to be teleporting uncontrolled until we figure this out."

Delinda studied Edric. "Do you at least have a reversal or something for it?"

"No…" He looked down at the toe of his shoe, which he ground into a flower petal on the floral printed carpet. "Like I said, it was supposed to be diluted. I didn't plan on anyone chugging it. You might be able to get one, though."

"What do you mean by that?" Delinda's eyes bored into him. "You caused this mess. You're the one who needs to sort it out."

"Yeah… about that… I've already got enough marks on my permanent record. If this gets out, they won't let me walk for graduation."

Delinda took a step closer to Edric. There was no way she was going to let him weasel his way out of this. "Sounds like *you*," she jabbed her finger at his chest, "shouldn't have been planning to mess with the punch bowl!"

He shifted away from her. "Look, I'm sorry about Tam… The potion shouldn't last more than a few hours. I think. And hey, I'm sure one day we'll all look back on this and laugh."

"Edric!" She warned.

There was a puff of smoke and the boy vanished, shrinking himself small enough to dash under the neighboring table.

"Oh, no, you don't!" Hazel hollered, snatching her magic wand from her purse and raising it over her head.

The commotion caught the attention of one of the chaperones. "Hey! You know the rules. No magic allowed on the premises! Put the wand away!"

"I… B-but he!" She motioned her free hand in the direction Edric ran.

"No buts, young lady."

"Yes, ma'am…" Hazel lowered her wand.

"Great. Now what do we do?" Delinda groaned, sinking into her chair.

Hazel sat next to her. "At least we know what's causing it. But what do we do about Tam?"

Delinda's phone screen lit up as it vibrated next to her elbow on the table. He sent her a thumbs-up selfie from the parking lot of Fry Friars captioned: *Teleported myself down!* "I told him I was coming to get him. Which reminds me, can I borrow your car?"

Her friend frowned. "My parents are really picky about who drives it. But I can take you."

After shooting Tam a quick response, she dropped her phone into her purse. "Are you sure you wouldn't mind? I'd hate for you to miss the banquet."

Hazel waved her off. "Girl, I know you'd do the same for me. We're *ride-or-dies*, remember? Besides, the mall isn't too far away. We should be back by the time they start serving, so long as Tam doesn't zap himself anywhere else."

Oof, there was that, too.

Delinda's dad was giving a police officer a ride as she and Hazel hurried across the parking lot. Seeing the patrol car parked nearby with its lights flashing, she figured someone must have called them on him for creating a disturbance. Again.

As Hazel drove, they conspired about how they were going to get back at Edric for this stunt. Delinda was content with ratting him out. Hazel, being one of the school's most talented witches, was more creative in her revenge plotting. She offered several curse ideas, like combusting homework, itching spells, or a hex to make his locker smell like sweaty gym socks for the rest of the year.

~ ~ ~

"I'm so glad you're here!" Tamil greeted them in the restaurant parking lot. He climbed in the back seat of Hazel's car looking tired and frazzled, his thick, black hair thoroughly mussed either from wind or him constantly running his hands through it. *Maybe both.*

"Edric planned to spike the punchbowl with teleportation potion, and your water bottles got mixed up on the limo," Delinda explained as the car pulled into a parking space to turn around. "You drank a full dose of it."

Tam rubbed the side of his face. "Seriously? Geez! Now it all makes sense. I'm lucky it didn't turn out worse."

"Don't worry. We're going to get him back!" Hazel assured him.

He leaned against the headrest and closed his eyes. "Awesome. But right now, I just wanna get back to the dance and—" The back seat went silent.

"Oh no!" the girls said in unison.

Delinda turned around, and, sure enough, Tam was gone. Her phone rang.

"Guess where I am!" Tam said sarcastically when she answered.

In the background came murmurs of a crowd and music playing. She pinched the bridge of her nose. "Don't tell me…"

"Yup, I teleported back to the dance. Gee, why didn't we think to do this all along?"

"Because we didn't know what was going on! You're lucky you didn't end up on *that* roof, either. Teleportation is risky if you don't know what you're doing!"

Tamil sighed. "Fine, I guess. I'll see you when you get here, then?"

"Yeah, we're on our way." Delinda's finger punched the *end call* button. "He teleported back to the dance."

Hazel gave her a quick glance before turning her eyes back to the road. "Are you flipping serious right now? Geez!"

Delinda's dad and the crowd of admirers were gone by the time she and Hazel returned. Dinner had just started being served as they entered the hall. The lights were turned down low, except for a row over the buffet, highlighting the enticing spread. She'd been looking forward to this meal all week.

Tam was at his seat, forehead cradled in his palms.

She sat next to him, but he didn't say anything or look in her direction. "Is something wrong?" she asked, cautiously.

Remaining silent, Tam slid his phone over to her. On the screen was a close-up picture of him standing on the Fry Friar roof in his suit, holding a smoothie and looking dejected. She noticed it was tagged to him on her class's Faebook group: *Hey Tam, dis u?*

"Okay..." Her voice trailed off.

"Scroll down."

She did as he said, seeing the comments section full of captioned versions of the picture. A particularly snide one from his ex-girlfriend read, "The only thing smooth in this picture is the smoothie." Delinda clapped her hand over her mouth, breathing the words "Oh my..."

He turned to her. "As if being a GIF wasn't bad enough, now I'm a meme, too."

"It's not that bad." She struggled to sound positive. "Some of them are kinda funny." The *Whatcha got there?* reference with an ostrich edited in next to him was pretty dang clever.

Hazel cleared her throat and muttered under her breath, "Elf-boy sighting, six o'clock."

The three turned to see Edric standing at a nearby table, talking to one of his friends.

Tam was first to stand, followed by Delinda, then Hazel. With Edric's water bottle in hand, he started marching toward the teen.

"Please don't tell me you're going to whack him upside the head with it," Delinda said just loud enough for him to hear.

"I should," Tam grumbled. "But I'm not dumb enough to get in that kind of trouble over something this stupid." He reached up and tapped Edric on the shoulder. "Misplace something?" he asked holding the bottle in front of the teen's face as he turned around.

"Hey, Tamil," Edric said, nonchalant with a mocking grin. "Heard you took a little tour of the town. Glad you made it back in time for dinner." He plucked his water bottle from Tam's hand.

Delinda clenched her jaw and crossed her arms, fiery anger that burned as red as her hair rose in her face. "You know what, I think *I'm* gonna deck 'im."

Edric grimaced, taking a step back from them. "Heeey now... no need to get violent." There was an uneasy waver to his voice.

"What was in the bottle?" Tam demanded.

The students at the table watched the scene playing out in front of them with baffled looks.

Edric's eyes flitted from them to Tam and the others. "You guys think we can talk someplace else?"

"As long as you don't try another disappearing act." Hazel flashed her wand, which she kept discrete in the folds of her skirt.

Conceding, he held his hands up. "Alright, fine. You've got me. Let's just head over there and talk this out." He jerked his head toward a wall furthest from their classmates and chaperones.

The group of friends followed Edric, winding around tables and between chairs. When they reached their destination, he turned to face them.

"What was in the bottle?" Tam repeated himself, standing in front of Edric with his fisted hands on his hips.

In their near two years together, this had to be the maddest Delinda had ever seen her boyfriend. He was always so easy going, almost to a fault.

Edric glanced down at the Beastie Bards bottle still in his hand. "It was just a simple teleportation potion from Apothefaeries. As long as you don't concentrate too hard on someplace, you won't teleport there. It's no big deal."

"No big deal?" Tam fumed. "I robbed my favorite

smoothie place because of that!"

Delinda rolled her eyes. "Oh my God, Tam, you didn't 'rob' them. It was what? Five bucks? We'll pay them later and explain what happened." Sure, it sucked, but he didn't have to be that dramatic.

"It will wear off after a few hours," Edric argued. "Just keep your mind clear and you're good."

"No, I am not *good*." Tam air quoted. "I want a reversal."

Edric huffed a sarcastic laugh. "Heh, good luck finding one. Apothe-faeries is closed already."

Tamil tapped his chin, eyes drifting upward as he thought. "I think I have an idea." He reached into his pocket for his cell.

"What's your idea?" Delinda asked.

"Remember Alaric from the shrinking powder mishap over summer?"

That creepy black-market werewolf was someone she hoped to never see again. "You can't be serious…"

"Lind, I don't wanna be teleporting around all night. If we can get this settled right now, then it's at least worth a try." He scrolled through the text history on his phone.

"You still have his number?"

"I mean… why not? And it looks like we need his help again, so it was a good thing, right?" Once he found it, he began typing a message.

"That guy sells illegal magical potions and artifacts!"

Edric glanced around nervously, his hands still fidgeting with the bottle. "Well, this was fun and all, but it seems like you guys got it handled. I guess I'll be going now."

"Oh, no, you don't." Delinda stepped in front of him. Hazel backed her up by brandishing her wand. "If we're going for a reversal, then you're paying for it."

"What!" Edric snapped, then quieted when he noticed students from the nearby table staring. "If Tam wants a reversal so bad, why should I pay for it?"

"Because it was your dumb prank! Either you set this

15

right, or I'm ratting you out."

Hazel waved her wand in front of him. "And I know enough hexes to make the rest of senior year a living nightmare."

As Edric looked between the girls holding him hostage, the new message notification on Tam's phone buzzed.

He tapped on the screen a few times, his brow, which was wrinkled with worry, relaxed into relief. "He's got something for me. We can probably still make the end of dinner if we leave right now."

"Looks like I'm not getting out of this," Edric said. "How much is a reversal gonna cost me?"

Tam held up his phone to show him.

"Aw man! There goes my spending money for the senior class trip!"

They made their way to the parking lot, Hazel continuing to hold Edric at wand-point. There was a chill to the evening air, which caused goosebumps to form on Delinda's shoulders. She shivered in her sleeveless dress, wishing for a jacket.

Tam noticed and slid his off and handed it to her before he resumed typing in Alaric's address on GPS.

Delinda thanked him, sliding it over her shoulders. Already she felt a little warmer.

"I think I remember where to go, but I've got the directio—" Tam vanished once again.

Edric laughed. "Oops! Looks like he thought too hard again…" His laughter died down when he noticed the girls staring at him.

Hazel yanked the back door of her car open. "Get in!" She ordered.

Delinda's phone chimed. "Tam's at Alaric's apartment building. He's sending me the address." His message concluded by stating it was very creepy in the dark and begging them to hurry.

~ ~ ~

16

The car came to a stop in front of Alaric's derelict apartment building.

"Are you sure this is the right place?" Hazel eyed it wearily, putting her car in park. "My witchy senses are picking up a lot of dark magic vibes from this place."

Delinda puffed her cheeks. She still couldn't believe they were paying this guy a visit... *again.* "Yeah, this is it. Tam's already inside, so let's just get this over with."

At the intercom, which sat under a flickering streetlamp, she pressed the button for Alaric's unit.

His smooth voice crackled over the speaker. "Hey there, doll."

"Ugh! Do *not* call me that!"

Alaric chuckled. "Whatever. Come on up." The building's door lock clicked.

The same rickety steps she and Tam climbed last summer creaked and groaned underfoot to the third floor. Delinda led them down a hallway decorated with peeling golden damask wallpaper on an off-white background. *Or maybe it was that badly stained.* She didn't want to think about it too much.

"Room number 308." She stopped in front of the door, giving it one soft knock as per Alaric's strict instruction.

The door opened, revealing a familiar young man with sharp features and light brown, slicked back hair. "Hello again." His wolfish grin went stern as dark eyes fell on the other two teens behind her. "What are you bringing half a school dance here for?" He held the door open just wide enough for them to get by. "In. And keep your voices down."

Inside the apartment, Tam sat quiet and still, his focus straight ahead on the blank wall.

"Are you okay?" Delinda sat on the edge of the couch next to him, reaching for his hand.

He nodded. "Fine. I just don't want to accidentally warp anyplace else when we're this close to finally being done with everything."

Alaric shut the door behind them. "Enough with the

17

chitchat. I've got a dragon steak dinner waiting for me and big boy werewolf things to do tonight. So, pay up, and count yourselves lucky I'm not charging you an arm and a leg for coming into the office this late."

"You wouldn't literally charge an arm and a leg... would you?" Edric asked, his expression going from annoyed to worried as he reached into his back pocket.

"I dunno, kid. An elven boy and witch girl dropping by after hours and taking up my precious time..." Alaric flexed his hand into a fist, long black claws appearing in place of his fingernails. "As I've told your friends here in the past, us werewolves aren't known for our patience."

Edric pulled the money from his wallet. Hazel and Delinda ended up chipping in some, with the promise of getting it back. They made it abundantly clear to him that if he didn't, he'd never know another peaceful day of high school again. "Here." He plopped the cash in Alaric's outstretched hand. "Is everyone happy now?"

Alaric counted the bills, then stopped, looking up at Edric with an indignant sneer. "Nice try, Elf," he growled, shoving his hand at Edric for the rest. "Hasn't anyone ever told you to never rip off a werewolf?" His face and arms bristled with silver fur as he shifted partially into his werewolf form.

Delinda and Hazel scoffed in unison as Edric handed over the remainder of the cash.

"You cheat!" Delinda glared at him.

"I oughta turn you into the toad you are!" Hazel threatened.

Fur and claws disappearing, Alaric reached into his coat, pulling out a vial of pink liquid. He tossed it to Tam. "I believe we're done here."

Tam pulled the cork from the top and quickly drank it. He scrunched his face. "Ugh, why can't these magic concoctions ever taste good?"

"It ain't a fro-lixor, kid." Alaric zipped his coat and straightened it. "Now get moving. I don't wanna be here all night."

Delinda held up her hand to him. "Hold on, I wanna make sure it worked first."

Tam smiled. "I tried thinking about the dance and didn't budge!"

~ ~ ~

"Dragon steak dinners? Do you know how expensive those are?" Hazel asked as the group left the apartment building. They stepped outside into cool air. A breeze had started to pick up, tousling everyone's hair. "Rain is coming," she noted, rubbing at the goose bumps on her arms. "I can feel it."

Delinda hugged Tam's coat tighter around her as the two of them walked to Hazel's car. She took the front seat while the boys slid into the back. The car started and began to pull away.

"Let's just get back to the dance and never speak of this again." Edric reached for his water bottle left behind on the seat and unscrewed the cap, bringing it to his lips. "Man, I'm thirsty."

"Hold on a—" Tam reached to stop him, his hand hitting nothing but thin air as Edric vanished. "Minute..." He pulled his arm back. "Oh, that's not good!"

Delinda turned to stare at him. "Tam, what happened?"

Tam winced. "I, uh... never actually got a chance to dump that thing out. It still had the teleportation potion in it."

"Ha!" Hazel snorted, slapping her steering wheel. "Serves him right!"

Delinda tsked. "Hazel..."

"What are we gonna do?" Tam asked. "I don't think I have his number."

Delinda straightened in her seat, watching the scenery go by as raindrops began to hit the windshield. A smile crept on her lips. "I don't think there's anything we can do. He'll have to figure this one out for himself."

Judy Khadra

Judy Khadra grew up in Greenville, Texas, and attended The University of Texas. There she met and married her Palestinian husband. They moved to Syria after his graduation, where they lived for one year.

She is currently working on a memoir from her Syrian experience based on letters she and her family exchanged during 1962-1963.

She retired from an automotive company. While there, she worked for executives, managing their internal and external business correspondence.

After the birth of her first great grandson, she is now matriarch of four generations. Her greatest achievements are having accomplished children, grandchildren, and a happy new great grandson to love.

37 Cents

Judy Khadra

Today I found 37 cents in the washer.
I smiled, remembering the found money when
my children were teenagers wearing jeans.
I told them to be careful with their cash.

When a crisp, clean $5 bill emerged from the dryer,
I showed them what I had found.
My daughter promptly claimed it.
"Uh, Uh, was there a name on it? I found it."
"Mom, it's mine!"

In the next few years, I found 1s, 5s and 10s.
They never knew.
I told them to be careful with their cash.

When they left home there was no more
cash in the laundry.
Today I found "my" 37 cents in the washer.
I smiled... I had become the teenager!

Lazy R Ranch

Judy Khadra

Old Man Durango Whitaker Smith died—had a heart attack out riding fence lines with his cowhands. They brought him home draped over his horse. He left doing what he loved and returned home the way he would have chosen.

His family gathered, had the funeral burial in the family cemetery down the pasture way, and sold the ranch in its entirety as soon as they could. They wanted nothing to do with the Lazy R.

I bought the spread in a hurry. It bordered on my sister's ranch in south Texas with County Road 324 splitting our properties. When the 911 emergency system required all roads to have a name, CR 324 was returned to its original name of Henry Prairie Road. It was romantic, and no one objected.

Both ranches were part of the original spreads along gravel roads that connected into the Old San Antonio Road, called OSR by the ranchers. Eventually, the road tied into the King's Road, which locals believed was called that because it ran into Mexico to the King's palace.

Henry Prairie Road had run by an old Spanish Cantina until the great flood of '74 washed it out. The County came in and rerouted the main road some miles away to higher ground. The old roadway remained, and local patrons continued to enjoy their time. Although the road change began the demise of the Cantina, when the owner, Guillermo

Robles, died, so did the Cantina.

The ranch house was a Spanish-style hacienda with an ornate fountain, porticoes, and detailed carvings. I opened the door and was totally amazed at what remained. Everything! The family had looked at nothing. Even Old Man Durango's morning coffee cup was still in the sink. I missed him. He had been a mentor, teaching me to ride, shoot and herd cattle. He sent me off to college with sage advice, and I often heard his words guiding me in difficult situations.

I moved in and met with the Lazy R ranch hands right away. I wanted to retain as many as possible and assure them that I intended to continue Mr. Smith's legacy and reputation of an exceptional, successful working ranch.

Soon, I was breakfasting with them in the communal bunkhouse kitchen at least once a week, enjoying the camaraderie, and gleaning important information about the needs of the ranch and my employees. I knew they were wondering if I would change the name of the ranch. I didn't want to lose the spirit and prestige of the Lazy R, but also needed to put my identity on it, too.

It was during these breakfast mornings that stories continued to pop up about the Cantina. It became Lazy R property when the road was changed. Durango had never claimed it while it was still a local gathering place. There had been some wild drunken times and competitive shooting games out behind the building. When I heard the stories, I wondered that no one ever died.

The strangest story that came from my ranch hands was the music. They often claimed that they could hear La Cucaracha music when they were out herding the cattle to another pasture. They claimed to hear it most often wafting on the air as they moved the herd from the grazing pasture not far from Henry Prairie Road.

My ranch was over 10,000 acres, so the reality of random music out on the prairie seemed impossible. I heard the stories so often that I began to believe and to listen. There were times when I thought I could hear the music too.

When things became settled and more routine, I decided to ride out and inspect the Cantina. As I saddled up, Diego, my right-hand man, handed me a canteen of water, reminding me that the water in out-pastures was pure enough for cattle but not humans. He gave me directions but also wanted to go with me. I insisted that I needed some time alone and this would be it. I wanted to see the place sitting in silent sunshine and feel the energy there. Perhaps the structure could be salvaged for something useful.

My ride out was peaceful with the exception of a lone, scraggly coyote appearing in the distance. He stopped and watched me closely as I did him. He seemed emaciated. I wondered if he was diseased. I was glad that Diego had reminded me to take my rifle and handgun. I had been away at college for so long that I had forgotten some essential details.

As I approached, the cinder block building shone dingy white in the blazing sun. The old black and white sign with Spanish markings survived, lying broken, warped, and splintered near the front door. Gingerly, I pushed open the half-hanging carved door and stepped into the dim light streaking through the broken windows. Instinctively, I looked for a light source and found the master switch behind the bar. It worked! There were a few broken bulbs, but enough came on to softly illuminate the interior.

The original bar was dark, carved oak with images of men and women dancing. The beat-up old tables and chairs were jumbled, but still there. I grabbed a chair and sat, just to absorb the atmosphere. I was sad to see the place empty, lifeless and dilapidated. Energetic memories of the ranchers came to me with music, laughter, and dancing sounds. Closing my eyes, I could see the men and women moving to a Texas two-step, with the women's ruffled, colorful skirts flying in the twirling.

I saw Durango sitting at the table with me drinking a beer

and grinning. I remembered the last thing he said to me before I left for college.

"Lillian Rose Parker, one day you will own this land. Promise me to keep the Lazy R brand."

I wondered why he had called me by my formal name. I had always been "little Mustang" because of my scrappiness.

"Of course, Durango. I will," I said, doubting future ownership, but humoring him anyway.

One of my thoughts was how could the building be used? Could it be returned to its original use and once again become a joyful place full of tequila shots, music, and dancing? Times and people had changed. But I figured my cowhands would appreciate a close location to socialize and maybe the surrounding ranchers would, also. I decided to discuss the idea with them at breakfast the next morning.

Jolted from my reverie, I heard a large rumble in the distance, and loud music started peeling through the building. Looking around, I saw an old, beat-up, but beautifully painted juke box sitting in a corner. I started laughing. My ranch hands had been right. They had heard music. The heavy vibrations from pick-up trucks on Henry Prairie Road had caused the box to activate, even after all these years. Those old, internal mechanics weren't even rusted in the dry Texas climate.

The mystery of the music had been solved and I had seen my old friend and mentor. I smiled as I remembered his two favorite sayings.

"Don't squat on your spurs and never pee on an electric fence."

I had heard him tell that to new cowhands when they were welcomed into the group.

In my reverie, I realized the new, old name for our ranch, Durango's and mine. The ranch would be called "Lazy R Hidden P" ranch. It would make a perfect cattle brand to hide my "P" inside the "R."

I would keep my promise to him. His legacy would live on

as mine began.

Preparing to leave, I flipped the master switch off. Why was the electrical still working?

As I approached the door, a sun beam pierced through the broken window, catching my eye and illuminating the juke box.

I shivered when I noticed the juke box was unplugged.

Liza Young

Liza Young is a writer of poetry and short stories. She has been published in *The MacGuffin, Oberon Literary Journal, The Pinehurst Journal, Cellar Roots Special Issue—Metropolyesterday Dreams, Sterling Script,* and the anthologies *The Space Between, Facets* and *A Velvet Bridge,* and won several writing competitions. She has done readings at the Scarab Club in Detroit and the Detroit Opera House.

An Act of Contrition

Liza Young

It is the baptism of rain we long for. The light
staccato of droplets loosening the oils that captured
our sin, gluing it over our pores until we can't breathe.

The cleansing slide of water down arms that refused
entry, pooling between breasts on a chest that heaved
angry words, down to feet cemented in pride's hole.

Like worms finding the blade tops of grass, wishing for eyes
to see the eventual rainbow, our weakness blossoms
        in the cloud
cover, tears and sputtered calls for help lost in the breeze.

Animal Crackers

Liza Young

She hefts hardened hands across the table
speaking to the boy, not yet two,
the one who was a careless night,
a one night stand,
a trip to the health department.
Without emotion, eyes unblinking,
she swats the crocodile tears from his cheeks.

Hush. Stop crying boy.

His pencil thin arms bridge the gap
searching for the love nest,
the comfort of kisses like sponges
that sop up childish rain
and homeless pain.
Eyes unblinking, trembling with fear
he is deprived of a nestle against the warm breast.

Hush. Stop crying boy.

She slips her fingers into the ziplock bag
given by a shelter volunteer
filled with animal crackers—
in case he gets hungry,
in case there's no dinner.
Through his tears, without flinching,
one by one, she eats the rhino, the lion, an elephant.

Hush. Stop crying boy.

He can not reach the tiny heart buried belly deep,
or halt the hand that says
Stop or I won't
Self-control though I don't.
The little boy falls into her lap
stifling tears, and learning that animals eat
animals, and sometimes their young.

Julie Angeli

Julie is a children's writer experimenting with adult writing. Her children's stories have appeared in *Spider* and *Cricket* magazines. She has also co-authored two picture books and, more recently, is the author of the middle grade book, *The Pearl Inside.*

She is a member of the Society of Children's Book Writers and Illustrators, Romance Writers of America, and Writers' Rendezvous, a critique group associated with the Bloomfield Township Public Library.

She is a graduate of Michigan State University with degrees in Packaging and Finance. She worked for several years as a consultant with Anderson Consulting (Accenture) before taking time off to raise her children and pursue a career in writing.

Her hobbies include tennis, traveling, playing the piano, and paddle-boarding.

The View

Julie Angeli

"The view is incredible!" Molly's voice echoed down the canyon.

Rebecca looked up at her sister while dangling over the side of a cliff, clinging to a scratchy, gray rope, her feet numb from too-tight climbing shoes. Molly had insisted that Rebecca rappel down first, so she could coach her from the top. Now Molly loomed over the top of the ledge. "We're so high you can see for miles."

"I don't like heights." Rebecca squinted down at the rocky canyon, wondering how her sister had once again convinced her to do something that terrified her.

"The view gets even better as you rappel down and get closer to the treetops," said Molly.

Rebecca craned her neck to look up at her sister. "Seriously?"

"Come on. Rappelling is easy and perfectly safe."

"That's what you said about scuba diving."

"And that was a great trip. Right?" Molly's eyebrows bunched together.

Rebecca grunted as she tried to get a stronger grip on the rope. "Are you forgetting about the shark?"

"It was a baby shark."

"It still had teeth!"

Molly shook her head then gazed across foothills. "Look

to the west. The aspen are turning."

"Are you kidding me?" Rebecca looked down. Her head spun. "I'm coming back up!"

"No!" yelled Molly. "It's too late to come up. Watch Laith. He's on his way down."

Rebecca shifted her focus to Laith, a guy Molly had met at the climbing store and talked into coming with them. He looked like a cross between a surfer and Spider Man with his sun-kissed hair and acrobatic climbing moves. The rope was centered between his bent knees while he walked his feet down the rocks. Biceps bulging, he gripped the rope in his hands, while a dusting of chalk settled on his sinewy forearms.

Rebecca's cheeks warmed as she focused on mimicking Laith. She centered her rope and inched her legs down, looking no farther than the rock face in front of her.

"Look at the red roofs on the buildings," yelled Molly.

Rebecca looked down. Her stomach jumped to her throat, and she froze.

Laith sprung off the rock and landed beside her, eyes twinkling. "How's it going?" His smile lines etched into his perfect face like the cuts in the boulders surrounding them.

"Fine," Rebecca squeaked. She kept her eyes focused on him as she tried to stop her heart from pounding. A balsam-scented mountain breeze brushed across the nape of her neck sending cool air down her sweat-soaked back.

His foot was inches from hers. He had the hairless, defined legs of a cyclist. Her breathing calmed. Somewhere in the back of her mind, she thought she heard Molly yelling something about pine trees.

"Try this." Laith pushed off the wall with his feet and sailed away from the rock. His buttocks flexed against the sheer fabric of his skin-tight shorts.

He swung back in. "Rebecca." His voice was like velvet. "Try pushing off."

Her foot stayed cemented to the wall.

"It's okay," said Laith. "I'm right here."

She peeled her left foot off the rock. Her right foot slipped, leaving her twisting in the harness, hanging just out of reach of the rock. She groaned. Dangling again.

"I'm on my way down," yelled Molly. "Check out the rock formations near the base of the canyon. The quartz makes them sparkle in the sun."

Rebecca wanted to smack her sister, but Molly was out of reach, moving down the ledge and beating her to the bottom.

"Swing in and try again," said Laith. "Remember how I did it."

Rebecca remembered his butt and wondered if that would be the last thing she saw before somersaulting down the mountain. She loosened her death grip on the rope, took a deep breath, and pumped her legs like a kid on a swing. Her feet landed flat against the surface as she swung back to the rock wall.

"Nice," said Laith as he rappelled down next to her.

Her lips formed a smile.

"Wasn't that fun?" yelled Molly standing on the ground below her, nearly blasting Rebecca off the rock.

When she looked down, she realized she was only two feet off the ground. She'd made it.

Molly hugged Rebecca before she had a chance to take off her harness. "Becky, wasn't I right? Wasn't the view incredible?"

Laith leaned against the side of the rock and took his shirt off, his chiseled abs matching the rugged canyon wall.

Rebecca looked at him, gave her sister a squeeze, and grinned. "You were right, Molly. The view is incredible."

Amy Laessle-Morgan

Amy Laessle-Morgan is a poet and Sterling Heights native. She graduated from Oakland University with a bachelor's degree in Communication. When not writing, Amy enjoys photography, music, cinema, reading and traveling. She often finds solace between the pages of books or in stacks of vinyl records.

Amy's work has been published in the 2020 and 2021 editions of *Sterling Script: A Local Author Collection*, *Unsent Love Letters: An Anthology*, *Poetic Reveries Magazine* and *Gypsophilia Art And Literary Magazine*. She was also a featured collaborative artist for the New York City concert series *Sounds Rising from Words* and Landmark Books 2021 Annual Haiku Contest winner.

Driftwood Beach

Amy Laessle-Morgan

palm leaves part ways as we escape oppressive humidity
and depart into another world
ripe with mystery

into a landscape of gnarled and twisted trees
stricken by erosion,
their firm grasp uprooted
shrines of ancient driftwood lining saltwater shores

bare feet climb slippery wet vessels of time
steady beams above crashing opalescent blue waves
draw us closer
as we dance in the moonlight of our finest hour

seagulls scream warnings
as the ocean pulls back the hem of her seafoam garment
revealing beneath us
a delicate seashell laden beach
as rust-tinged horseshoe crabs play a fiddling melody
we stand upon the boundary of darkness and light

outstretched arms greet enchanted heavens
as we ascend sun-bleached thrones of pine
surveying the beauty within the graveyard of trees
adorned with rose-colored sunbeams
paying homage to life's counterpart

everything grand must come to an end
but somehow your cleverness escaped this fate
preserved with a salty-aired kiss,
resting eternal bedded down upon the sands of time

If We Make It Through the Night

Amy Laessle-Morgan

if we make it through the night,
will we wake again with eyes wide shut
to grey-blue haze of unpromised mornings
that blend with precision into monotonous routines

in that moment, will we hold ourselves accountable
hold our own hands, hold the child whom we lost,
hold the door open for unattainable truths and reconciliations
into unknown chasms of all we have lost and who we are
    now

if we make it through the night,
if it is possible, if it is plausible if it is precedent,
do we have the charisma to bind our souls together,
to love and cherish one another,
to not leave anyone behind

anxiety penetrates through deep caverns of our existence
can we break the cages that imprison our hearts and minds
will we see the gift that lay ahead of us is time and yet time is
    lost,
we have lost so much time,
so much,
so many

if we make it out of thick blankets of charcoal fog
into rolling hills of spring eternal
I hope to find you there, once again, before all of this
if we make it,
If we make it through

Mary Rose Kreger

Mary Rose Kreger lives in the Metro Detroit area with her family, where she writes fantasy for teens and blogs about her spiritual journey: before, during and after the convent. Mary is writing and recording her convent memoir on her author website, www.maryrosekreger.com. She also contributes regularly to www.monasteryinmyheart.com.

"The Left-Handed Warrior" and "A Midnight Meeting" are excerpts from her young adult fantasy novel, *Avalon Lost*. All of Mary's works, both fiction and nonfiction, are stories of healing and hope.

The Left-Handed Warrior

Mary Rose Kreger

Will Owain panted for breath and tightened the left-handed grip on his sword. They'd only started fencing practice in the Sacred Wood an hour ago, but he was already tiring.

"Don't let your guard down, Will. Unless you prefer to begin Journeymen's Training with a few missing appendages."

Raven sure means business today. Even after a month of training, this isn't as easy as it looks.

The King's Watch had granted Will permission to work one-on-one with Raven before joining his fellow journeymen in October. They'd focused on strength training, especially as Will's injured wrist continued to heal.

Will was grateful for this chance to prepare. He knew how much his father, Lord Madoc, wished to have him at Gwynedd Castle this time of year, learning the ways of a young prince. Still, when Will visited home to ask his permission, his father had not refused him.

"Go back to the Watch, and with my blessing," he had said. "Yet do not forget your poor father, who waits for your return."

Will could no sooner forget his father than his throbbing right arm. He would never have left him, if it weren't for this new chance to rescue his mother.

Curse the black day that made me choose between them. Will wiped the sweat from his eyes and watched Raven's movements. *Curse the hour that tore my family apart.*

Zing!

He ducked as Raven's next attack swung where his head had been a split second before. He stumbled over a few tree roots to retreat from his master's lightning-quick offense.

An opening!

He sucked in a breath of pine-scented air and swerved his blade up to meet his master's shoulder. The blade just grazed Raven's watchmen insignia, an image of an owl clutching a blazing torch.

"First blood," Will gasped, lowering his arm a bit.

Raven struck him with the hilt of his sword. "We're not finished."

With his right cheek still stinging from Raven's blow, Will raised his guard again and whipped out a Romantic stance at his opponent's torso. When Raven began to parry, Will lifted his blade, drove his master's sword into the ground, and brought his blade up diagonally across Raven's now vulnerable chest.

"Better." Raven's eyes darted behind Will's shoulder. "Now say there's a second enemy, behind and to your right."

With one fluid motion of his left hand, Will slung his sword into his belt, pulled out his hunting knife, pivoted and threw the knife inches deep into a tall cedar behind him.

Strong arms wrapped around his neck and chest. Will felt the point of a knife jabbing into his ribs.

"Now say I miraculously survived your deadly attack," Raven whispered into his ear.

Will twisted his body weight to one side, pried the knife out of Raven's grasp, and sent his right boot crashing into his opponent's toes. He used all his remaining strength to wriggle himself free and step back a few paces from his master.

Despite the coolness of the forest air, sweat poured down his temples, stinging his eyes.

Raven regarded him thoughtfully. "By this point, your unstoppable opponents may have noticed your injured arm. They may try to exploit your weakness."

With a nimble movement reminiscent of a panther, Raven launched himself towards Will, aiming his attack at Will's bandaged right arm. When he pulled his arm aside, Raven grabbed it and sent Will reeling into a bed of pine needles.

But Will drew his sword as he hit the ground and pointed it at Raven's throat. With his *left* hand.

"It's not my weakness anymore." He glared at his master. "It's my strength."

Raven stood still and quiet above him. A ray of morning sun slipped through the dense cover of the Sacred Wood, lighting up his dark locks and catching golden flecks of color in his otherwise pure brown eyes. Like Will, Raven was of average height and slighter build. A stranger couldn't have judged how dangerous he was by his looks alone. But Will knew how strong and deadly his master could be, when he chose. Will had fought him a thousand times and more, and never once had he felt like he'd defeated his master.

Raven offered his hand.

"We're all finished for today," his master assured him.

Will seized his hand gladly then, and let Raven help him back onto his feet. He shook off a few pine needles and squinted in the sunlight.

"But we've hardly even started."

"You don't need any more practice. Four weeks of training with your left hand, and, as you said, you've already made it your strength." He clasped his apprentice's shoulder. "You're ready, Will."

"Ready for what?"

Raven's eyes shone. "Ready for a new mission." He smiled mysteriously and clasped his apprentice's shoulder. "And ready to prove yourself, to someone who can change things for you."

A Midnight Meeting

Mary Rose Kreger

Will wrapped his cloak around him as he watched the moon rise over the Academy. Faith's treehouse, constructed many yards up an ancient Scottish oak, afforded him the best view on the grounds. From its roof, Will could look east towards the mansion, north towards the gymnasium, south towards the stables, and west towards Pine Mountain. The treehouse also offered him a relatively comfortable place to rest and practice his watchman skills.

All the same, it gets a bit lonely up here.

Dylan, Laurie, and Philia took turns bringing him meals, but other than their food runs, Will was alone.

A single figure skittered across the moonlit lawn before disappearing beneath the tree canopy below. Will slung down the trap door into the main room of the treehouse, then tiptoed to the gap in the wooden frame that served as the treehouse entrance. He clutched his hunting knife, which he and Dylan had recovered along with the Avalian swords, just in case his visitor was less than friendly.

"Will?" A pale hand clung to the treehouse floor.

Will hurried forward and smiled down at his guest. "Philia! Welcome." He held out his hand and helped her climb from the rope ladder into the treehouse.

"Whew, that's a long climb." She shrugged a large satchel off her back, undid its clasp, and pulled out Will's new favorite food.

"A sandwich," he sighed in gratitude.

Philia grinned and pulled out another. "Brought you two, just in case Laurie's late with your lunch tomorrow. And some water bottles, apples, protein bars, et cetera…"

He laid out a plaid blanket on the floor, and they both sat down for an impromptu picnic. Will devoured his sandwich while Philia munched on an apple and told him about her training.

"Mum opened up my sword bundle for me today. Inside was this amazing left-handed sword called *Brightwind*." Philia held out her left hand, wriggled her fingers in the moonlight peeking through the treehouse slats. "You're left-handed, too, aren't you, Will?"

Will rested his head against the opposite wall and shook his head. "Not by nature. Just by stubbornness, I suppose."

She blinked at him curiously.

"I broke my right wrist during my last watchman's trial," he explained, flexing his right hand. "My master Raven wanted to send me home to my father, but I told him I could learn to fight with my left hand just as well."

"Raven?" Philia drew her knees up and rested her chin on top. "As in, my Uncle Raven?"

Will nodded. "He's wonderful, Your Highness. A first-rate watchman, and the best of mentors. You'll like him, I promise." He smiled. "Raven seems to think I fight *better* with my left hand. Maybe I should've switched before taking the last Trials."

"So, what are these Trials?"

Will grimaced. "It's the test all watch-apprentices must pass to become professional watchmen. Journeymen, they're called."

"Oh, that's cool," she said with interest. "I'd love to watch one of them."

He glanced at her and took another bite into his sandwich.

"Are they very hard to pass?" she continued.

He chewed and swallowed, then raised a wary eyebrow at her. "Princess Philia, there are times when you can be very tenacious. Has anyone ever told you that before?"

Philia slid her feet down and clapped her hands on her jeans. "Someone might have mentioned it." She wagged a finger at him. "But don't change the subject. I asked you a question, and you clearly don't want to answer. So now I have to know. Are the Trials hard?"

Will shifted his position on the blanket. "Yes. No. *Yes.* For me, they are. I know all the skills, and then when it comes time to perform before the judges..." He lowered his voice. "I fail."

The princess bobbed her head in understanding. "Stage fright."

Her words surprised a smile out of him. "I've never heard that expression before."

"Plenty of people get nervous before a big performance," Philia explained. "I was so jittery during the school play last year, I botched half my lines opening night."

"It's...it's more than just nervousness." He picked at the remains of his sandwich. "My mind starts racing, and my heart gets to pounding. I remember how high the stakes are, and forget everything else."

"Poor Will." She paused for a moment.

Will imagined her mind whirring, producing new questions in the silence.

"Why are the stakes so high at the Trials? I mean, your father is a prince of Avalon, so you already have a trade besides being a watchman, yes?"

He took his time before answering her.

"I wanted to become a watchman so that I can save my mother." It physically hurt to speak the truth out loud. "She handed herself over to Amaranth at Flaxen Grove to save my father's life." He avoided Philia's eyes, focused instead on the

49

swaying tree branches outside the treehouse. "Some of the King's watchmen have come close to rescuing her. I've trained hard these past five years to follow in their footsteps, and bring Fiona home."

Fiona still walked in his dreams these days. Sometimes she laughed and embraced him; most times she sobbed and wept. Even now, he could hear her haunting cry, whistling across the floorboards and sweeping through the great oak.

Come and find me, Will.

He wrenched his gaze away from the open door. He was startled to find Philia sitting beside him, only a hand's breadth away.

"Dear Will. You must have a lot of your mother in you." Her warm fingers brushed against his arm.

He stiffened, and she pulled her hand away.

"Sorry," he said. "It's just...Hamish said almost the same thing, the last time we met."

"What happened that night? I—it almost seemed like he was going to," she breathed, left the words unsaid.

"Like he was going to kill me?" His tone was flat. "I think he meant to, at first. But he changed his mind." Will hesitated. "It happened after I told him about Fiona. About her sacrifice. I told him, and then he said...what were the words? 'You're very like your mother.'" He shook his head in frustration. "I still don't understand it. After that, he let me go free."

"Is that *all* you said?"

He closed his eyes a moment and rubbed his forehead. "I told him anyone could change. I told him he could become a man worthy of honor again." *Like my father Madoc.*

"Do you really believe that?"

By the Founders, all her questions!

"I—I don't know. No. Yes, Hamish could change." Will dropped his arm, caught a sliver of his reflection in a mirror hanging across the room. He lowered his eyes. "I have to believe people can change, Philia. Otherwise, what hope do I have for myself?"

"You touched him, Will." She locked eyes with him, as if daring him to contradict her. "Something about *you*—not just what you said, not just about your mother—made Hamish choose good when he planned to do evil. That's the power you have, worth far more than a devastating right hook."

Will had to smile at her precise description of Hamish's attack. The Princess knew her hand-to-hand combat.

"Perhaps. Whatever the reason, I am glad."

"Dear Will," she repeated. "You have a power in you, far greater than you know. A selfless purity."

She extended her hand, traced the bruise around his left eye, the cut above his ear, the row of stitches on his neck. Her touch was electrifying. Waves of longing rippled through him wherever her fingers landed. He yearned to close those inches between them and kiss those sweet, perfect cherry lips.

Philia dropped her hand into her lap. "You helped me bring my mother home. I—I want to help you bring your mother back, too. Maybe I can talk to my father about it when we get to Avalon." She turned two earnest eyes on him, swept a swirl of chocolate hair behind her delicate ear. "There must be something we can do to bring Fiona home."

"Thank you," he whispered. She was so lovely in the twilight. Even in the darkness, her presence glowed.

If only I could capture an image of her, as she is right now, and keep it forever. Then I should always be happy.

This thought was accompanied by a fierce sting of guilt.

And what of your poor mother? Can you ever be happy while she remains Amaranth's slave?

Philia was observing him. "You watchmen are brimful of secrets," she said. "Will you tell me someday, what's going on inside that fierce mind of yours?"

He dared to reach out and kiss her cheek.

"I can tell you that you make my mission here quite easy.

You are lovely as Bright-Eyes, Starman's Daughter, from the early days of Avalon."

Philia smiled. He liked the dimples that appeared in both her cheeks. "I better go home now, or Mum will start to worry."

He nodded. "I'll follow your movement from above, in case there's any trouble."

She stood up and placed her empty satchel over her shoulders.

"Hey Will?"

"Yes, Your Highness?"

"Mum wants me to learn the High Avalian Stances with *Brightwind*. Do you think you could teach me?"

"Of course," he said with a bow. "It would be my pleasure."

She grinned. "Awesome. Meet me in the church cemetery tomorrow at midnight. I know the perfect place to practice."

~ ~ ~

At midnight, Will emerged from his hiding place amid the church's weathered stone walls. Philia gasped when she saw him appear, as if from thin air. Then she seized his hand in her own and whispered, *Come*. Her eyes gleamed like jewels in the moonlight.

The Princess drew him along the short-cropped lawn to a shallow indentation in the wall. She shifted the fallen leaves that had caught in the culvert, revealing a door. After a few tries of the lock, it groaned open. They both winced at the sound.

"Let's go." Philia ducked her head under the low doorpost and ventured inside.

Will followed. She gently took him by the arm and led him down creaking steps to a long, narrow space filled with glowing lights.

"I blocked the windows up with curtains and duct tape this afternoon," Philia said. "No one should see a thing from the outside."

The basement, which Will had expected to be covered with dust, was surprisingly clean. The stone floor was scrubbed and polished, the walls free of cobwebs, and orderly candles lit up the long space.

Will had only weeks to teach her what he'd learned in fifteen years, so he didn't waste any time with small talk about the room's cleanliness. "You know the Avalian Stances, Your Highness?"

"I've seen them in Mum's books."

He walked backwards three steps, settled into an open space free of candles and shelves. Then he drew *Llewgalon* from the pack he'd strapped to his back. Its spring green blade shimmered in the candlelight.

"These are the High Avalian Stances. With these twelve stances, you can complete any move, counter any attack, defeat any enemy. The actions are simple, but their mastery is not. Each stance has such power, but a warrior must give himself over to that power—understand it, know it, practice it—in order to unleash it." His Gwynedd fencing instructor had taught him this lesson since he was three years old. "I've far from mastered them, but let me show you all the same."

He brought his blade to center. "The Perfector." He flung his blade to the right with deceptive abandon. "The Giver." His blade drew back to center. "The Worker." Now his sword slashed across his body as he pivoted on his right foot. "The Romantic." He continued to go through the moves, ending with a full turn and a quick stop. "And...the Encompasser."

She bobbed her head, pressed her lips tight. "Again." Her hands dropped to her sides, and he watched her fingers flick in time with his movements.

He repeated the motions, calling each one as he slipped from one stance to the next. He knew these moves like Raven knew his bow, as his father knew Gwynedd, as the shore knew the sea. They were a part of him. He was always Will, but when he fenced he was *more* Will.

"Again!" She pleaded, her eyes picking up everything, absorbing his every move.

He moved so fast now, the strokes blurred into one, the Encompasser stance zinging through the space with deadly speed. Will sucked in a deep breath and wiped his brow. "Your turn, Your Highness." He handed her a wooden practice sword.

Philia clasped the sword with both hands, just as Will had done. She paused a moment, muttering the stances under her breath.

"Ready? Begin!"

Her arms sprang into action. First one stance, and then another. Will studied each stance as she let them fall. It was her first turn, but she got the sense of all twelve of them. She added a certain feminine grace to the strokes, and a swiftness that Will might have envied, were Philia a fellow watchman.

"The Encompasser," she whispered, laughing a little when her foot dragged on the final turn. Her face lit up with joy. "Amazing, Will. How'd I do?"

"As good as any beginner could on their first try." Will made some adjustments to her footwork and corrected the angle of her hands and elbows. The more they practiced, the more he respected her ability to learn. She anticipated his corrections, asked intelligent questions, and seemed neither too elated nor dismayed by his praise and critiques.

"When you shift from the Worker to the Romantic, it's meant to be a surprise," he explained, demonstrating it for her. "Change the timing, every time."

"Of course. If you're predictable, you're dead," she stated cheerfully. She repeated the two stances, changed her timing by a half-second, even added a miniature feint that caught Will off guard.

"Good. If we were fencing just then, I would have

blocked you at the wrong time. You could have stepped in and struck me here." He tapped his chest.

"I could have pierced the lion's heart," she teased.

He blinked. Lion-heart was the English translation for *Llewgalon*, his father's sword. "You know Welsh."

"Well, I grew up in Wales, didn't I?" She raised her sword, and he parried it. "Now teach me how to do this better, so I don't get stabbed through the chest before I see my father again."

"As you say, Your Highness." Will lifted his sword into the Perfector stance. "Again!"

~ ~ ~

When they were finished, Will and Philia rested on an old wooden bench and shared a flask of water. Their elbows bumped together when she passed him the water, making the Princess giggle.

Will smiled. Her joy was contagious. He could drink from it all day, without tiring.

"So, you're in the Watch," she said dramatically. "What is that like? What kind of songs does a watchman sing?"

"When we're working, we don't sing at all. We wouldn't be very good watchmen if we kept making noise all the time."

She must've guessed he was teasing her, because she laughed even more. "No, seriously," she pleaded. "Please, sing me one of your watchman songs. Mum told me about them." Her face fell a little when she mentioned the queen. "She said they were beautiful."

And how could he possibly resist such a request?

"As you wish, Your Highness," he nodded his head in deference. "This one's named 'Watchman's Calling.'" He closed his eyes, remembering. "I learned this one when I first began my life as a watch-apprentice, wandering the still pine groves of Avalon." He paused for effect, and then he sang:

> *I have walked, far where men hath never trod*
> *Lonely shadows hunt me down.*

I have laughed, deep within the vaulted wood
There is a land where shadows die.
I am altered, but her hand does not break me
Through Bright-Eye's hair, the violet and the blue.
I have fought, may the dark never take me
As I go to pierce the shadows of the night.
In the shadows of her hair all shadows die,
In the shadows of her hair...all shadows die.

Will felt the heart of a watchman locked in these words. A restless desire, a lonely calling. "This song tells the legend of Ranger and Bright-Eyes, two of the founders of Avalon long ago."

Philia lowered her head and rested it on Will's shoulder. He was startled by her touch, but he didn't pull away.

"Tell me about Bright-Eyes, Will," she said. Her breath still smelled of strawberries and vanilla. "Tell me how she makes those shadows die."

Shadows. In their midnight hiding place, there were plenty. A sealed basement at a late hour: this was their dominion. Still, the room's candles burned on, casting soft radiance on Will and his fair companion.

"I suppose... Bright-Eyes focused on the light. On the single pin-prick of light in the darkness." He grew more confident in his theory. "That's how she found Ranger long ago, yes?"

Philia considered his words. "I think so. The tales say they first met at night." Her forehead gently brushed his ear. His arms ached to hold her close.

"My mother first told me this story as a boy," he said. "How Ranger and Bright-Eyes were true lovers, and how after many trials and difficulties, their love became the Northern Lights that grace the Gwynedd skies."

She raised her head to smile at him again. "Then it must be true."

Kalle Kivi

Kalle writes mostly about actual experiences of real people in today's modern world. Yes, there are exaggerations. No, there are no compromises.

"Free Will" is based on an account as told by his sister upon her recovery from a surgical procedure.

Kalle finds inspiration and support from the Sterling Heights Creative Writers' Workshop and the Shelby Writers Group. His poems can be found in Sterling Script 2018, 2019, and 2020.

He is a graduate of the University of Michigan and Utica High School.

Free Will

Kalle Kivi

The long tunnel dark, mysterious
in ways I could not
Feel
Nor think clearly of

Passageway walls inviting, and yet
appearing to disappear
all the while
I am compelled to journey

with taste of colors, a smell
of direction of peace
ever conscious
of some pull I am twisting, floating

Toward destination pinprick of light
growing beauty color kaleidoscope
When
I am stopped, some force

Before computer screens, ledgers infinite all around
electric fantastic confusion
"What,"
I am asked, "Are you doing here?"

I don't hear these words, rather I feel
"There's been some mistake; you're not
meant
to be this far yet; so go back now"

When I awake I don't recall any journey
back to this here today, but
real voices
Tension, concern in my nurse's dark eyes

"Karen," the cardio doctor calls near
Are you all right? Your pacemaker
STOPPED
But the defibrillator kicked in

Just like it was supposed
To do   ....

Rebecca Eve Schweitzer

Rebecca Eve Schweitzer is a writer, artist, editor, social media consultant, marketer, zine maker, and word nerd based in Metro Detroit. She has an overactive imagination, hordes books like a dragon, and would like to be a unicorn or phoenix should she ever be forced to grow up.

She is a member of the Sterling Script editorial board, a founding member of the Tuesday Morning Writers, and an active participant of the Sterling Heights Creative Writing Workshop. Her writing, art, zines, and blog can be found at www.beccaeve.com.

I'm going to be late today

Rebecca Eve Schweitzer

A spider accosted me in the shower this morning
Disguised as a bit of mildew
or some wayward hair
it clung to the grout lines in the corner

Blurry-eyed and behind schedule
I considered leaving it
I gathered my courage, pushed
The drain cover aside with my toes

Then curled them under my feet
to protect them from the small dot

I directed the stream of water toward it
watched the speck come to life
as eight tiny legs clung

First to the wall then to the top rim of the tub
It scrambled for safety as the whirlpool twisted
closer and closer to doom

Finally, it tucked its own vulnerable appendages
under its tiny black body and braced itself

I watched as it swirled
around the drain once
twice, thrice
then into darkness

I uncurled my toes
replaced the drain cover
and shivered

Whether from the narrow escape
Or the premeditated murder
Before my morning coffee
I don't know

The terrible truth about peace

Rebecca Eve Schweitzer

The thing no one tells you
    about the peace that passes all understanding
    Is that it doesn't come alone.

It sneaks in with the shock
    The sudden crying fits
    The moments you can't catch your breath

It clings to you as you crumble
    From the inside out

It rides along to distract you
    When you notice that life keeps moving
    Even though you are certain the Earth
    Stopped and shattered

That's the thing no one tells you

The peace persists
    whether you want it to or not

The peace carries you across the bridge
    as it breaks behind you

The peace won't let you drown in the river
    no matter how much it feels like
    you want to
    need to
    should

And the worst thing no one tells you is
    that the understanding doesn't come
    that the puzzle never fits together again
    that this is what the peace is for

Teresa Moy

Teresa Moy is a technical writer, editor, tai chi and qigong instructor, and lover of learning. She graduated from California State University, Sacramento, with a degree in English.

Her first published short stories appeared in *Sterling Script: A Local Author Collection*, and she won first place (memoir category) in the Rochester Writers Contest 2021. "Soup and a Good Luck Knot" is a companion short story to her novella, *Chasm Awakening*.

Teresa is a member of the Sterling Heights Creative Writers Workshop. She enjoys sampling new cuisines, hiking Michigan's beautiful state parks, and dreaming about exotic lands far away.

Soup and a Good Luck Knot

Teresa Moy

Mei's fingers worked the cord, folding one loop over another and creating a crown for both sides of the red, good luck knot. The intricate design emerged as she created the basket-weave center and floppy petals. If she made it tight and even, maybe luck would fetch her a husband before she turned thirty.

Someone cleared his throat, and she flinched in her chair.

A young man leaned against the counter with his milky, flawless skin creased into a scowl around his lips.

"I'm sorry, I was..." she stammered, setting aside the knot.

"Busy playing around and not paying attention?" He paused, his eyes scanning her from top to bottom. "I'd like some seaweed soup, *please,* if it isn't too much trouble."

"Um, yes. I mean, it isn't too much trouble. I'll... go get it now. For you."

Steam from the large wok moistened her face as she peered into it. The soup wasn't quite ready, but she ladled it into a bowl and rushed back to the counter. The hot soup sloshed out and burned her hands. Cheeks flushed, she wiped the bowl and handed it to the man. As he took it, his fine, soft hands almost touched hers.

She sighed and gazed out the front window, past the customers crammed in the small dining area, past the layer of humming conversation and soup slurping that hung in the air. In the park across the cobble-stoned public square, children chased each other, and men laughed while they played board games. A small group practiced tai chi, stepping together and extending their arms like one breathing body while a musician played his flute. If Mei ever had that freedom, she didn't remember it. She'd grown up in her parents' restaurant, serving meals and using the cash register as soon as she was able.

Glancing back at the young man, she soaked in his almond-shaped, brown eyes and chiseled jawline. She hoped he liked her soup, because that might be all he'd like about her. Her mind juggled ideas for clever conversation, but everything sounded stupid. Noticing the red knot on the counter, she swept it into her pocket. This one she had made well. It had to bring her good luck, even if the ends were frayed from constant knotting.

"Stop fooling around," she could hear her father say. "A pretty knot won't bring in the money."

"Or find you a husband," her mother would add.

Chiseled Jawline flung his spoon and chopsticks onto the counter, frowning at his bowl. Mei hoped he hadn't found a hair or anything worse in his soup.

"I'm sorry. Can I…"

"This is horrible!" he exclaimed. "Not the seaweed soup I'm used to. Give me something else."

She hastened into the kitchen. When she returned with some noodles, he glared at her.

"This is… on the house?" she said, attempting an awkward smile.

"Well, it should be," was his curt reply. "And I want to speak to the restaurant owner. I have business with him."

"Oh, he's busy in the kitchen. But, um, I'll tell him. He'll be a bit. Okay?"

After delivering the message to her father, Mei grabbed

the garbage bag and shuffled out to the alley, tossing the bag into the metal bin. She grimaced at the benevolent, cheerful sun. *I sounded like an idiot,* she thought as she sat on the bench and buried her face in her hands. *I'll never find a husband if I can't talk to a man.*

A few yards away, a gentle and confident voice interrupted her solitude. "The energy you emit will be the energy that returns to you. Instead of focusing on what you do not want, focus on what you *do* want."

Mei lifted her head and shaded her eyes. The voice belonged to a man with a shaggy black ponytail and a burlap bag. She couldn't see his face. His companion was a young lady with round, wire-framed glasses. Between them, a couple rolls of fabric leaned against the brick wall.

"Easier said than done," replied the woman, blotting her cheeks with a handkerchief.

"Allow your attention to rest on what is desired. Intent is a powerful thing," said the man, shouldering the fabric. As the two departed the alley, his voice trailed off. "And it is available whenever you choose to use it."

Mei froze, thinking how she had changed the course of her future with a dreadful vision—her fiancé, Rong, shivering in his bed, his face as white as the porcelain pitcher on his nightstand. His breath turning into wispy, swirling clouds. His mother wailing when his ghost slipped away in the darkness of night. *It's only a bad dream,* she had assured herself.

Weeks later, when a sinister illness had crept into Rong's body, Mei frantically wrestled with the dire images lingering in her mind; if she could subdue them, maybe they'd surrender. But her focus vitalized them, and they kept rising to the surface and bobbing on her consciousness. As her husband-to-be expelled his last breath, his heartbeat silenced forever, she knew he had died because of her.

She fingered the red knot in her pocket, drew in her breath, and exhaled with renewed resolve. Even though her betrothed had entered the spirit world, she hoped her true husband still traversed this one.

She returned to the kitchen, to the aroma of fried noodles, oils, and braised meat. With a rhythmic motion of her cleaver, she minced garlic, chopped green onions, and cut ginger root into matchsticks. Scooping up the pieces, she tossed them into the boiling broth. She whisked eggs and dribbled them in, using chopsticks to swirl them into feathery strands. The sheets of dry seaweed crackled as she tore them into strips and dropped them into the soup.

I need a kind and loyal husband, she whispered, staring into the wok. *Someone who understands me. Someone who sees me.* The bubbles expanded like frog vocal sacs before popping energetic sprays of broth into the air.

"Where have you been?" sneered her father with his hands on his hips. "I've been looking for you."

"I took out the garbage…"

"And you decided to goof off while you were out there? Your break isn't for another two hours. So, forget about it now. You've already taken it."

When she extended her hand to explain her brief absence, he swatted her arm away, flinging it into the side of the steaming wok. She yelped from the searing pain and rushed to the sink to run cool water on her injury.

"Get out there! Our customers are waiting!" Her father turned off the water and pushed her toward the door. Mei stumbled out, biting her lower lip.

An older man stood at the counter. His rough hands and tanned skin advertised he was a laborer, possibly a farmer or field worker. He wasn't particularly handsome, and his disheveled hair made him look like he'd just awakened from a good nap.

"How may, I mean, welcome to our restaurant," said Mei in a monotone. "How may I help you?"

"I'm not sure. What do you recommend?"

Mei thought of her red, threadbare cords; her father had promised her a small allowance if she sold enough soup. In a voice soft enough for Chiseled Jawline not to hear, she said, "Um, seaweed soup? I mean, I'm making it right now. Almost done, a fresh batch, that is."

The farmer paused. "I'm usually not a fan of seaweed, but I'll try it."

He continued staring at her until her cheeks reddened. "Are you okay?" he asked.

"Yes. Yes, I'm fine," Mei lied, pulling her sleeve over her injured arm.

The farmer sat at the other end of the counter from Chiseled Jawline. He squeezed himself between two portly, bald men, one chowing on dumplings and the other slurping up noodles. He took off his straw hat and placed it in his lap.

As Mei set the soup before him, he pointed to her pocket and asked, "What's that?"

"Oh, nothing," she said, shoving her red knot out of view. "May I see?"

She hesitated and then took it out. He examined her handiwork.

"This is very nice. The loops remind me of dragonfly wings. I don't have the patience to make stuff like this."

Mei bowed her head, mumbled a "thank you," and left to wait on other customers. How could he compliment her knot? The cord was fraying and discolored. There were spots where she had tied the ends together because they had torn apart. But his words lightened her mood.

~ ~ ~

While the full moon hung in the sky, the farmer emerged in Mei's dreams. He was yelling at her, and his words burned into her arm. She fled, racing toward a dark shadow pressed into the earth. Her apron strings flapped in the wind behind her. Her braid came undone.

Mei awoke and bolted upright, her heartbeat pounding.

Was this another premonition?

She examined her singed forearm and recalled her father's indifferent, remorseless countenance. Somehow, even though the kind farmer had materialized in her dream, she must have been reliving her father's punishment. That was the only logical explanation.

~ ~ ~

"It's time you moved on," grumbled her father. "You'll be thirty soon. We can't have you hanging around here like an old spinster."

Mei bowed her head.

"Just one more mouth to feed. One more person to clothe. How much soup did you sell today?"

"I… I think I sold enough. Maybe I could buy some more cord for…"

"No!" he said, slamming his hand on the table. Mei jumped. "You did not sell enough soup. And even if you did, I wouldn't let you squander it on something as stupid as red cord. Waste of time! Waste of good money!"

She headed to her room, suppressing any facial protests until after she'd gently closed the door behind her. Just two red cords. Or only one. Not much to ask for a tiny slice of fun. Hearing her parents' voices down the hall, she tiptoed back to the door and cracked it open.

"It's so unfortunate," her mother said, shaking her head. "I guess since we matched her with Rong at birth, Mei's never had to look for a husband. She doesn't know how to talk to the opposite sex. If only she wasn't so… awkward. Should we ask Auntie Shan for help? She can find a great prospect from another town."

Her father put a finger to his chin, thinking. "What about that young man at the restaurant today? He wanted to print menus for us. I told him the blackboard was fine and shooed him out. Anyway, he left a business card, so I can ask her to check his background."

Mei mulled over this prospect. Chiseled Jawline as her husband? At least he was easy on the eye and close to her age. Maybe his rude behavior stemmed from having a difficult or stressful day.

"Good idea. That's a start," said her mother.

As it turned out, Chiseled Jawline was an excellent match. Mei's parents cried with joy and hugged each other when Auntie Shan gave them the news, and they asked her to arrange a meeting.

He hates my seaweed soup, thought Mei. *But he's good looking. We should have handsome babies.*

"He goes by the name of Bo, and his family lives a couple villages away," Auntie Shan informed them. "His parents have been searching for the right girl, but he's very... picky."

During the meeting, Bo's parents outlined his accomplishments. He was educated, intelligent, and had a good head for business. Soon, he could run the printing shop on his own.

Mei pictured Bo as her husband. Sharing a home with him, making babies. With a gorgeous man walking beside her, she'd be the envy of the women in town. Her heartbeat fluttered.

When Bo entered the room, his face fell. "Oh, it's you? I thought you were someone else."

"You can't afford to be so finicky," pleaded his mother. "She's a lovely girl."

"She can't cook, and she's lazy, clumsy, and dull."

After Bo's family left, her father's chilly rebuke deepened her shame. "You will have to refine your social skills if you want to land a husband."

"It isn't my fault he's so picky. His parents said so," she answered. As soon as she uttered these words, she regretted it.

"Insolent girl!" he growled, pinching her ear hard between his fingers until she winced. "You're lucky Auntie Shan is willing to help you find a suitable husband! We could throw you to some lowlife drifter to get rid of you, you know."

Outside of his line of sight, her mother shook her head slightly.

~ ~ ~

The farmer with the tanned skin returned to the restaurant. He took off his straw hat, smoothed his hair, and headed for a counter stool. Mei greeted him with a nod, noting that today he wore a clean, buttoned shirt.

"You're back again," she said. Realizing her words might sound rude, she added, "I mean, welcome back. What do you want? I mean… can I take your order?"

"Do you have a recommendation?"

"Um, pork belly? Pork belly noodle soup? It's… popular," she said, wiping her hands on her apron. She retrieved the order pad from her pocket.

"You know, I enjoyed the seaweed soup very much. Your recipe, perhaps?"

Mei studied the pad of paper in her hand and fiddled with her pen.

"Well, then," he said. "I'd like some more of your specialty. By the way, I'm called Gen."

She murmured her acknowledgement.

"And you are?"

"I'm… I mean…"

"Slow down," said Gen. "I'm not in any hurry. Just take a breath and then tell me."

She sighed. "I go by the name of Mei."

"Ah, a plum blossom," Gen said, smiling.

"A what?"

"Plum blossom. The meaning of your name."

As the lunch crowd packed the restaurant, Mei flitted from table to table. Her father was in a foul mood, barking orders and complaints from the kitchen. Embarrassed, she flew around the dining room to satisfy his every demand.

After Gen left, she glanced at the counter spot where he'd been, and beside his tip and empty bowl was a hint of red. She hastened to clear his dishes and gasped at the red cord tied into a bundle with string. Her heart leapt with joy. Peering out the window into the public square, she saw his stocky figure a block away. She brushed the unexpected gift into her pocket.

~ ~ ~

Auntie Shan arrived the next day with news of another match for Mei. "This man, he may be quiet, but he's thoughtful and moral. He's a strong, earnest worker. We must go to them, though, because the mother is bedridden."

They traveled to the next town to meet him. Auntie Shan approached the house while Mei and her parents waited outside.

"Stand up straight," her father snapped at her. "Smooth your hair. And lower your eyes. Don't stare at the house like a twit with your mouth hanging wide open…"

His reproach faded as muffled, angry voices rose from within the house. Doors slammed. Mei's parents looked at each other with raised eyebrows.

Auntie Shan returned, her mouth drooped into a pout. "I'm sorry. The family has changed their minds."

"What?" exploded Mei's father. "We didn't even get to talk with them!"

A faint movement by the upstairs bedroom window caught Mei's eye—a flash of a long, black ponytail before the curtains were yanked shut. *He didn't even give me a chance to ruin the meeting with my bumbling personality*, she thought. *He had taken one glimpse and knew I wasn't good enough for him.*

Back at home, Mei dragged her feet to the courtyard while her parents and Auntie Shan discussed new plans. Through the open window, she heard her aunt exclaim, "I will not fail her! I will find her someone."

A pair of chattering birds flitted and circled above her as

they built a nest in the loquat tree. Mei's dream of building a family of her own—with rosy-cheeked children tugging on her apron strings, begging to be picked up and cuddled—scattered in the soft breeze like wispy dandelion seeds. She laid her hand on her chest, felt her heartbeat, and wondered how it knew what to do, yet Rong's had not.

She thought about the meeting Auntie Shan had set up when they were teenagers. Mei had served tea to Rong and his parents, and she had liked his long, moppy hair hiding his shy eyes. The image of his boyish face burned in her memory from that only encounter.

Here in this courtyard, they had met. Here she'd accepted his proposal. And here she'd heard he was gone. A guilty tear slid down her face and rolled into her mouth. She tasted its salty sadness.

Whispers of the old saying for a long marriage echoed in her mind: "A bamboo door should match a bamboo door; a wooden door should match a wooden door." Where was her match? Maybe she didn't have one anymore.

~ ~ ~

"I have another marriage prospect!" said Auntie Shan, her eyes twinkling.

Mei sighed and shook her head. What would be this man's excuse for rejecting her?

"He claims he made an offer, and she's already accepted him!"

"What?" said Mei's father, choking on his tea. His head whipped in his daughter's direction.

She returned his gaze with her own surprise. "I don't know who she's talking about…"

He slapped her. "Don't lie to me, child! Where is this boy you've been sneaking around with behind our backs?"

"He goes by the name of Gen," said Auntie Shan. "I checked his background, and he's a decent match."

Gen? The tanned-face farmer with the messy hair who

liked her seaweed soup? He had made no offer, nor had she made any promises to him. Mei looked from Auntie Shan to her parents. He was too old for her, possibly fifteen years her senior. And what did she know of farming? She was a restaurant girl.

Mei wracked her brains to make sense of this assertion, and she figured it out. In a small voice, she said, "He came to the restaurant twice. The second time, he left me a bundle of red cord, and I took it."

"That's not a proposal!" cried her mother.

"Who does this man think we are? Fools?" Her father raised a dismissive hand. "Trying to trick us into this union? He can't be trusted."

Mei thought back to the other day, when her father had threatened to send her off with the next nomad who wandered into town. Perhaps he loved her after all.

"His ways may be odd, but give him a chance," said Auntie Shan.

Gen arrived on time for the meeting. Mei cracked open her bedroom door to spy on him as he stood stiffly in a dark blue, Tang-style jacket. She watched her aunt introduce him to her parents, and her parents welcome him with polite, reserved manners. He bowed his head as he presented them with tea cakes and a fruit basket, apologizing that he didn't have anything better to offer them.

She stared at her face in the mirror, at the foreign makeup plastered on her lips, cheeks, and eyes. This time, she wore a silk *qipao* that used to be her mother's. The side slits only exposed her legs up to her knees. She admired the hint of plum blossoms embroidered into the fabric.

When her mother came to fetch her, Mei smoothed her hair and glanced at her lucky red knot—she'd hung it in the southwest corner for love and happiness. They headed out to the courtyard where everyone was seated and waiting to have tea. She took tiny, dainty steps and kept her gaze lowered, but she still caught the beam in Gen's eyes.

"You look lovely, my dear." Auntie Shan gave her an approving smile.

Gen said he was a rice field worker and would provide a wonderful home for Mei. His parents had passed away years ago and left him a large parcel of land.

"I don't, um, understand," Mei said, almost more to herself than to him. "How…" She fell silent.

"It's okay. Take a breath and tell me when you're ready."

She studied her hands trembling in her lap. "How was I to know… accepting the red cord. It was a marriage proposal?"

Gen smiled. "You weren't. I only told your aunt that so I had a fighting chance. A woman like you wouldn't be available for long."

Her father accepted this reason with a slight nod; her mother remained skeptical, her mouth set in a tight grimace and her arms crossed.

Mei poured tea for Gen and handed him the cup on a saucer. "Why me? I mean, you don't know anything. About me, that is."

"Your red knot. It shows you have perseverance and patience. Your refusal to take credit for your seaweed soup—which I do love, by the way—shows you're humble," said Gen, sipping his tea. "Besides, you're the prettiest woman I've ever met."

He gazed at her until she blushed and turned toward her mother, whose face had relaxed.

When he finished his tea, he pulled a small, embroidered red bag from his pocket, placed it on the saucer, and slid it toward her.

What man still honors such an old tradition? But Mei understood the bag's meaning, so she dared not touch it yet. She stole a quick glance at the rice field worker with his rough hands and crinkly eyes—a plain laborer who liked her seaweed soup and ability to make a good luck knot. She'd muttered and stumbled through every conversation with him, and he hadn't cared.

Dear Rong, she thought, *is it time for me to let you go?*

She looked up at the birds in the nearby loquat tree. Their nest was complete, and she could see the tiny eggs they were fiercely protecting. She drew in a long breath and exhaled even slower. Picking up the red bag, she fingered the intricate embroidery and smiled at Gen. Her future was sealed.

The Mentor

Teresa Moy

You walked to class in nut brown Birkenstocks,
Elbow patches affixed to your sport coat,
Your watch discreetly placed in your open textbook.

Quiet voice revealing a relentless curiosity.
Thoughts churning behind your poet eyes
That crinkled when you smiled.

I silenced my naïve mind and noisy vocal chords
The better to absorb new ideas like a cotton ball.
I imagined there was hope for me.

When you took me under your wing,
We studied women warriors—
The hidden, glorious, brave, shunned, and smothered.

You then asked for my voice
But I, a warrior, had slashed my own tongue,
My sword dripping with unworthiness.

As my inert words lie on the floor of my chest
You threw them a sturdy rope.
Battered and timid, they shakily grasped it.

They clambered up the walls of my throat,
Valiant soldiers pressing onward with clenched teeth
Out of the trenches, into the light.

Now, you have flown, clutching the shadows of your heart.
Through a tiny window, curtains half drawn,
My glimpse into your world, frozen.

So embrace your song of peace
Lingering, soft and gentle, in a vineyard sunset,
Floating like eastern cottonwood.

I have learned to flutter, glide,
And sometimes soar with my wings.
I can speak now. *Arigatou gozaimasu.*

Kathleen Belanger

Kathleen is an Oakland University graduate with a major in English. Her last position before retiring was with Mastercard as a senior technical communicator. She is a mother of five and grandmother of ten.

Kathleen enjoys creative writing and has participated in several critique groups throughout the years. Two of her short stories were runners up in annual short story contests sponsored by Oakland University for graduate students and alumni.

Kathleen currently participates in a critique group associated with the Sterling Heights library.

To a Ghost House

Kathleen Belanger

I trace your timbers between the maples
In an outline over embers,
Recreating in my mind
The porch with sagging steps,
The damp cellar, and
The kitchen where I found
Grandma with her currant jam, warm bread,
Fortunes in tea, and stories,
The mysteries of the attic,
Old clothes in trunks, secrets in old diaries,
Kerosene lamps, a victrola.

Now you're a ghost like the man from Ohio
Who came with his bride and cleared the land,
Raised your frame with the logs he split
Planted wheat and raised his family
Years before my time.
I will look for you in the pages
Of a dusty album of photographs,
Tuck you away with old memories,
And tell my grandchildren stories
Of summers I spent on the farm.

Sister

Kathleen Belanger

She rolls in the morning mist
And pops out of the sky
In her bedroom sometimes
At noon
In the fierce sunshine.

She follows long shadows
In the late afternoon
And travels on the edge
Of a broken dream
To a starless midnight.

My Dandelion Romeo

Kathleen Belanger

Soft-petaled roses sent parcel post
Wrapped in green tissue
In the traditional congregation of a dozen
Deliver love's message
With the passion and charm of Cyrano.
I take a deep breath
And feel some disturbance
In the rhythm of my pulse.

But love has another flowery messenger,
The pert and sunny dandelion.
Bunches of them come on summer days
In the fist of my four-year old son,
Slightly crushed with enthusiasm.
When I put them in a vase with lots of "ooohs,"
And place the perky blossoms
On the kitchen table,
I feel as warm as melting butter.

John Stockdale

John writes fiction and is currently working on short stories. Two of these stories were included in Sterling Script 2021. He has also written a memoir about his time at the U.S. Naval Academy. He is an active member of the Sterling Heights Creative Writers' Workshop and the Bloomfield Township Writers Rendezvous writing group.

In a previous phase of his life, John was a business valuator and wrote numerous articles for professional magazines and a technical book. At that time, he was also the owner and publisher of a newsletter publishing company.

John's hobbies are writing, sailing, hiking, and fishing. He feels lucky to live in Southeast Michigan and lucky to live with his wife of fifty-three years.

The Girl in the Red Crown Vic

John Stockdale

In the summer before my senior year, a family moved into the big house with the pool, and their daughter drove a '56 Crown Vic—red. The first time I saw her, she was driving by our house with her windows open and her long hair streaming. I was a young man in love.

The first day they moved in, the Crown Vic girl, name of Sandy, joined into our nightly teen conversations, which included tons of jokes I did not necessarily want my parents to hear. Sandy never told any jokes, but things she said came out saucy, always said with a smile that invited me in and promised a good time.

My boring life was about to take a huge step up. So high, I'd be with the satellites the U.S. was hurling into space. This was going to be a summer to remember.

~ ~ ~

My parents had this stupid rule that every night the family crammed into our kitchen for supper at six o'clock sharp. It seemed to me their purpose was lecturing us on morals and good behavior. A smart dude like me knew their words did not apply in the modern world, so I played a song on continuous loop in my head to drown them out. Just before supper, the DJ had played the golden oldie, "Sandy," by Larry Hall, and that was my current selection.

"Skip, did you hear me?"

"Sorry, Dad, I was thinking that practice will start soon, and I'll begin with a bang like one of those rockets NASA's launching into space."

"Son, hear this loud and clear."

Oh boy, what he said without fail when he figured my soul was on the straight path to hell.

"These new neighbors of ours. Seems they've got a lot of money, and it's bad news giving their daughter her own car to drive."

"Girls should never wear red, or drive red," Mom added. "This girl is headed for trouble. You've always stayed on the straight and narrow. The last thing we need is you getting into hot water with a floozy. Don't you get into that car."

The evils of the wealthy was an everyday topic, but the immorality of girls in red was a first.

"This girl acts loose, and your mom's right about her flaunting red. I don't like giving orders to a guy turning eighteen. But you stay out of that car."

~ ~ ~

I was edging the walk the next day. The lawn needed mowing, but grass creeping on concrete wouldn't bust it up.

Sandy pulled up and flashed her sassy smile. "Hey, Skip, I've got an errand to run, and I could use your company. We can do some talking and whatever."

This was it. She'd invited me into the vehicle of red evil. And, boy, did I have some ideas about the "whatever"!

I dropped the edger and jumped in the car.

The very first rule in the club of teenage males is that the driver of a Crown Vic should burn rubber. But she eased the car forward, shifting the gears as gentle as rocking a baby.

"Soft lift off." I gave her the look of an all-knowing instructor. "This kind of car ought to have squealing tires."

"Skip, here's a tip about girls." She winked. "We don't like jack rabbit starts. Take our time. A slow lift off."

"Oh yeah?" This was going to be a day to remember.

"Where are we headed?"

"Weekly task from Dad I used to hate. Now it's not so bad except for driving by myself. You're solving that issue."

"Fair exchange." I laughed. "I'm not edging the walk."

The car went quiet. The only sound was the Four Seasons playing *Candy Girl*.

"I just got a job at Kentucky Fried Chicken," I blurted out. "I hear they're looking for girls, too. I think you ladies make a dime an hour more than my ninety-five cents just for ringing up the cash register."

Shoot, this chick didn't need money. I'd blown it sky high.

"Cool beans." The racy smile danced on her lips. "I'm real good at ringing it up. Plus, Dad's on my case about chipping in for gas and oil. And, if I had a job again, he might not find so many errands."

My foot wasn't in my mouth. And I was ready to get her errand over and move on to the "whatever."

She turned into this rundown old building with a bunch of cars parked in front.

"Hop out, Skip, and help me load the goodies into the car."

I couldn't figure out what a racy chick from a rich family was doing in a place like this. Some kind of illegal activity? Was I headed for that trouble my folks had lectured about?

When we walked through the door, she flashed that smile of hers at the older fella behind the counter. "Hey, Bruce, you got the goods?"

What the heck? She flashed her come-and-get-it smile at old dudes, too?

"Miss Sandy," he said, "yours are ready. Five today. I'll get 'em out of the back."

"Only five." Sandy turned to me and said, "We'll be done in nothing flat. I know a place we can sit in the shade, have a nice chat, and a good time."

I didn't like dropping off drugs, but the rest sounded

great.

Bruce dropped the good-sized packages on the counter.

Dang, this was dope delivery big time.

~ ~ ~

When I got home that night, parental supervision came down on me like Russian atom bombs.

"You rode with her," Dad said. "What I told you not to do. Grounded for a month."

"She pulled up in that red car wearing a red blouse," Mom said. "Double red means double trouble. Let's hear the shenanigans you got into."

I looked her straight in the eye, real arrogant, not a hint of the initial disappointment I'd felt. "Delivering meals-on-wheels kind of shenanigans. Then we sat in a park laughing and talking about our high schools. Then pushed kids on swings. Turned out to be the best time ever and with a really nice girl."

Dad lit a cigarette. Mom got up, filled her coffee cup, and sat back down.

Dad blew out a long stream of smoke. "Okay, grounded for a week."

Mark Morgan, Jr.

Mark Morgan is a Detroit native, teacher, and poet. His work is featured in *Angry Old Man Magazine*, *The Rising Phoenix Review*, and previous editions of *Sterling Script: A Local Author Collection*. Mark also won Landmark Books' Fourth Annual Haiku Contest in 2018.

When not teaching or writing, Mark may be found reading, practicing martial arts, or listening to jazz.

Stardust Reunion
after The Doors

Mark Morgan, Jr.

Virgo's lips still scorched from Leo's kiss
                                while asters waved Hello
in sync with midday's fervent sighs.
                        clustered hydrangeas bowed as I
approached you, witnesses to our
                        stardust reunion. that late summer, love
echoed the smoldering germination of
                        the cosmos that swallowed us. you
took my hand and smiled, guided by
                        sunflower sentinels. there won't
ever be another moment when the light
                        and breeze stroke their white hair as you
wrap an entire universe around your finger.
one day, we will rest upon a bed of conquered winters, tell
stories to regale the chrysanthemums.
                even then, your eyes and freckles will remind me
of the sunflowers' tawny countenances
                        as they blessed desire and destiny, and your
laughter will plant seeds that remind me
                        of the day you took my name

Behind September

Mark Morgan, Jr.

children bound along a swinging bridge
with no regard for the plodding shake
of their parents' knees. they learned early
that the best way to hear each plank's creak
is barefoot, beneath chaste bones and flesh

the kids didn't care when the car stalled
on the way to Disneyland. the lure
of a roadside safari made them
giggle as they poked bloated raccoons
and flattened turtles with newfound sticks

when the groan and hiss of school buses
creep behind September sunrises
rows of waxed floor tiles will scuff beneath
the tremor of single-file fault lines
and the rumble of starving spirits

Susan Dudgeon

Susan Dudgeon has worked hard all her life. After a long day at two jobs, she would lay in bed at night and write funny or poignant stories in her mind. She was too tired to get up and put pen to paper. By morning, she'd forgotten them. Now, as she is on the downside of this mountain called life, she has the time, the discipline, and the energy to write all the stories and fantasies that fill her heart.

She writes, volunteers, goes to lunch, swims and suns. She loves her little dog, Georgie, and all the new "great" babies that are her family's fourth generation. At the age of 68, life has never been better.

Grama Jane

Susan Dudgeon

Grama Jane lived in her marital home on top of her mountain until she couldn't anymore. She grew up in a time of no phones, no cars, no tractors; the horses did the heavy work. She was the only midwife for miles and professed the "blessing of birthing babies" was her calling. Grama Jane was my great-grandmother.

As a proper woman of the Baptist faith, she wore a house dress and an apron every day. Her thinning white hair reached the floor. She combed it from the ends to the scalp, much like grooming a horse's tail. She lightly patted talcum powder through her tresses. With bobby pins wobbling between her lips, ready to secure her hair, she rolled it up into a bun. She twisted it into place like a magic trick. As a girl, I asked her to do it over and over so I could watch, but she would only do it once.

All her life, Grama Jane called Grundy, Virginia, her home until moving to Michigan to live with her son, Garnie, and his wife, my Grama Elsie. When I married, I lived down the road from my grandmothers.

One Sunday afternoon, I walked over to visit them. Grama Jane, dressed in her Sunday dress, good apron, and street shoes, sat on the sofa with pocketbook in hand as if she were waiting for a bus. Her wheelchair sat near the front door.

"Grama? Are you going somewhere?" I asked her.

"Levi Johnson is comin' for me. He's takin' me down to the Foot Washin' Meeting," she stated.

"Hmmm?" I followed the scent of cornbread baking and turnip greens simmering into the kitchen to find Grama Elsie.

"Grama Elsie, who is Levi Johnson?"

"He lived down in the hollow. When Jane couldn't get down the mountain anymore, he used to pick her up for church and run errands, chop wood, that stuff."

"Is he here? In Michigan?"

Grama Elsie shook her head and chuckled. "He's dead."

I went back into the living room and sat down beside Grama Jane. "When is Levi supposed to pick you up?"

"He's comin'," she said.

"Grama, tell me about Foot Washing Meetings?"

"We go down to the crick that runs behind the church meeting hall and wash each other's feet. We humble ourselves. Like Mary Magdalene did for Jesus. You've never been?" She shook her head with a look that said, "Tsk, tsk."

I went back to the kitchen, pulled out a dishpan from under the sink, and put a squirt of lemon Dawn dish soap in it. As the pan filled with warm water, tiny bubbles floated up and popped in my face.

Grama Elsie smiled at me as she eyeballed the cornbread in the oven. "Almost done," she said.

"There's nothing better than a warm piece of buttered cornbread and a cold glass of milk." I carried the dishpan to the living room, tip toeing to avoid splashing water all over.

On bended knees, I removed Grama Jane's shoes and knee-highs. Placing her feet in the pan, I cupped the soothing water in my hands, let it run down her calves and ankles, and began washing her feet.

"Is this right, Grama?"

"Yes." She nodded, waving her hand for me to keep going. She rested her head on the back of the couch and closed her eyes.

In that moment, it was hard to imagine she had ever been pretty. Her face was criss-crossed with deep wrinkles, eyes sunken with facial bones jutting out. Her skin was translucent. Splotchy red and brown patches splattered across her forehead and cheeks. The sun had kissed her face too many times.

As I massaged her feet, she started to hum her favorite hymn, "Stairway to Heaven."

"Grama? Do you think Mary Magdalene trimmed Jesus' toenails when she washed his feet?"

"I believe she did."

While she quietly hummed, I trimmed her nails and cascaded the warm water down her frail legs. I dried her feet and rubbed lotion into her cracked skin.

"How about if we put some nice white socks on to keep your feet warm and soft? You don't need those knee-highs back on. It's getting late, Grama. I don't think Levi's going to make it."

She stared straight ahead and said, "He'll be here."

I got a pair of cushioned socks and wiggled them on over the resistance of her arthritic bones.

She stretched her arm out, reaching for me. "You're a good girl, Dana."

I smiled and squeezed her hand.

I'm not Dana.

L. Broas Mann

Broas Mann received Mechanical Engineering degrees from Illinois Institute of Technology and Northwestern University. That was followed by a fifty-year career at Chrysler Corporation engaged in automotive research, during which time he wrote many technical papers and reports.

Upon retiring, he wanted to continue working with words and ideas, so he turned to writing historical fiction and published four books, three journals of Levi Broas, about the history of his family's pioneering adventures in western Michigan, and *The Journal of Ruth Ann Broas* about the journey from a woman's perspective.

Mann also wrote *On and Off the Road*, an anthology of trips in North America and Europe that he and his wife Marion enjoyed.

The Storm — Part Two

L. Broas Mann

After wreaking havoc in the Gulf of Mexico on several of the working oil rigs, the hurricane that had been dubbed "Jane Doe" moved north. As she passed over the dry land of eastern Texas, she lost some of her ferocity but retained the massive charge of warm water. Upon crossing into Oklahoma, Jane encountered a mass of cooler air sweeping down from the northwest. She welcomed it like an old friend.

OKLAHOMA
TULSA—APRIL 20, 1969

George Altmann's Teutonic lineage had gifted him with a six-foot four-inch, 245-pound frame, and being a single-minded, hard-charging guy, people and things tended to get out of his way. As he left his father's Tulsa real estate office that steamy April afternoon, he had only one thing on his mind—revenge.

He jumped into his Ram pickup and roared out of the parking lot onto Route 117. George's destination was the Glen Oaks Country Club, and his purpose was the absolute annihilation of Brian O'Halloran. George and the feisty redhead had attended Oklahoma University on scholarships from the same high school, and had been close friends for years. But on the golf course they were arch-enemies.

In last year's final outing, Brian had humiliated George. Many of the club members were in the bar when they returned, and Brian had broadcast the news of his one-sided victory. In his thirst for today's revenge match, George had postponed two closings and a client meeting.

Leaving the office, he didn't notice anything particularly ominous about the sky. But even if he had, he was so hungry for this year's first contest that he was not about to allow anything to interfere, not even weather.

Oklahoma's reputation as a breeding ground for violent storms is widely known and feared. Cool air flowing down from the Rocky Mountains overrides warm, humid air pushing its way northward from the Gulf of Mexico.

Now, when it comes to air and water, Mother Nature has a strict rule—the hot stuff belongs on top of the cold stuff. So, by late afternoon, these pockets of warm, moist air along the ground began to punch their way up through the cool layer. As the water vapor in these rising columns mixed with the cool air above, it condensed and gave off tremendous quantities of heat to the upper atmosphere. These monstrous "heat pumps" did a great job of cooling the earth, but they also added a lot of energy to the upper level winds that were already very strong. These booster shots turned them into violent storms.

On Friday, April 20, there was a deadly squall developing along a line from Fort Smith to Wichita. It would pass directly through Tulsa, which included within its corporate limits the Glen Oaks Country Club.

~ ~ ~

By almost any standard, George Altmann was a handsome man. Short blond hair, piercing cobalt blue eyes, and a dazzling smile, but his appearance was not the only reason he was a successful realtor. He grew up in this very competitive business, learning the ropes from his father. But the older man hadn't just taught young George how to sell property—

he'd taught him how to sell people. He became a shrewd negotiator and a great "closer," with a knack for getting potential buyers and sellers onto a middle ground and closing the deal by the sheer force of his personality.

And, he approached every venture the same way, even a golf match.

GLEN OAKS COUNTRY CLUB

Glen Oaks is a challenging course, set on rolling hills near the southwestern Tulsa suburb of Jenks. As Polecat Creek winds its way to the Arkansas River, one of its feeders meanders around several holes, often to the consternation of club members. But, on this day, it would be the weather, not the creek, that raised the golfers' hackles.

"Get ready to eat a big piece of humble pie." George's eyes bore into his opponent as he needled Brian on the way to the first tee. "I'm going to blow you away today."

"You may have a lot of help, you big windbag, especially on the first three holes." Brian brushed away an unruly shock of red hair—the perfect complement to his round, ruddy face. He was nowhere near as big as George, but Irish belligerence made up for his smaller stature. His ancestors had been almost wiped out by the potato famine. The few who survived immigrated to America, but ethnic hostility made their lives almost as hard here as it had been in Ireland. So, at an early age, Brian had to become a fighter to survive in a family beset with hardship and conflict, and he carried those traits with him into adulthood.

"That wind out of the west should offset your monster slice on a few holes," he said, "but on the rest you're all mine."

Brian was right. On the first hole, George timed his tee shot at the peak of the wind gust, and it flew 280 yards, landing dead center in the fairway. A good middle iron put him on the green about eight feet below the flag. Brian, on the other hand, because of his considerably shorter drive, found the creek on his second shot. The penalty stroke cost him the hole.

With another great drive, George took the second hole, too, as Brian struggled from tee to green. But, when they approached the third tee, Brian noticed a distinct shift in the wind, warmer and now out of the south. Competitor that he was, he said nothing, hoping his partner would not detect it.

Flush with victory and pleased to have driving honors again, George addressed the ball as he had on the first two tees. His mighty swing, and the newly developed head wind, resulted in a very bad slice deep into an out-of-bounds field adjoining the third fairway.

"What the hell?" George exploded. Smiling inwardly, Brian again said nothing, but corrected his own stance and swing for this change in the wind, and hit a respectable shot in the middle of the fairway.

George took a drop in bounds, hit a great recovery shot out of the rough but missed the putt, so the penalty stroke cost him the hole. On the fourth, a short par three, Brian could hardly conceal his glee as he sank a long curving putt to even the match. After that, the lead alternated back and forth, and they were still tied by the time they reached number thirteen.

Now, even George could see the huge thunderheads building rapidly in the southwest and heading their way, but he was determined not to leave this match at a draw. He needed to regain the lead to assuage his bruised ego, even if they couldn't finish the round. "I've lived in Oklahoma a long time, and I've seen a lot of these storms," George said. "Judging by the lightning and thunder, that front is at least twenty minutes away. We've got time to play thirteen and fourteen, and that gets us back near the clubhouse."

Brian retorted, "I'm not sure of your weather wizardry,

but I guess we can make it that far."

By now, the warm Gulf air had created several moisture-laden columns. They were rising swiftly through the cooler air that swept out of the Rockies and over the Texas and Oklahoma panhandles, feeding the storm along a one hundred-mile front. The prevailing winds were driving it on a northeasterly course at over sixty miles an hour, so, when George and Brian agreed to play two more holes, the front was really less than ten, not twenty, minutes away.

NUMBER FOURTEEN

The creek swallowed both drives on the thirteenth hole, and they each took a bogey five. Then, just as Brian hit a long drive off the fourteenth tee, a vicious lightning flash seemed suddenly closer. They considered driving directly to the clubhouse, but at this point the difference between casual golfers and addicted competitors became apparent. They decided there was time to finish the hole.

They might have made it but for George's slice.

"Damn," he said, "that one could cost me the hole and it was my last Titleist. Well, it's in bounds and the rough's not too bad there; I can find it."

"George, the rain is starting; I'll buy you a new ball—let it go! We'll finish the match next week." But this is where the "closer" took over—George would not let it go. He drove their cart into the right rough and quickly found that the ball was playable. He picked a six iron from his bag and was at the top of his backswing.

As it raced over the countryside, the squall line was building an intense negative charge in its thunderheads. Following it on the earth's surface was an equally intense positive charge—its "electrical shadow"—climbing over all the obstacles in its path. This shadow was seeking a shortcut to its negative brother in the clouds. The head of a metal golf club about seven feet in the air was ideal.

Brian regained consciousness rather quickly. It was strangely calm where he lay on the wet ground, but there was turmoil all around. He was numb, both physically and mentally, but he knew he had to see if George had been hurt by that sudden blast of hot air. He just couldn't get up the strength. "Not yet. I'll lie here and rest a minute."

When, finally, he could stand, the rain and wind had picked up again. He struggled to George's prone figure, and what he saw stunned and sickened him beyond belief—the melted golf club—the burnt clothing—the blackened face.

Brian was still on his knees, sobbing, when the greens keeper found him a few minutes after the storm had passed.

.

Marie Thrynn

Marie Thrynn is a domestic poet who dwells in Michigan and the land of anxiety. She grew up in the Sterling Heights library and prefers the company of books.

Stop sending me flowers

Marie Thrynn

Stop sending me flowers.
i don't want to watch anything else
wither and die.

petals fall in fading colors
plucking, pruning, preening,
pretending pretty corpses
have more time if i treat them kindly

a reminder that i can't save everything
and i have to let go.

Katy Hojnacki

Katy Hojnacki works with paintings, illustrations, novels, short stories, and even comics to delve into fantasy worlds. She is a writer, avid gamer, artist, and illustrator of the children's book *I Can See With My Eyes Shut Tight*. As cover designer and artist for *Sterling Script: A Local Author Collection*, she also contributes her writing and editorial skills to the publication.

A graduate of Oakland University with a degree in English and Studio Art, Katy is an active member of the Sterling Heights Creative Writers Workshop as well as the Tuesday Morning Writers.

Brewing Dreams

Katy Hojnacki

Byron pulled on the heavy wooden door to the taphouse. Ms. Killian had managed to harvest an old, elaborately carved door for the front of her establishment. The deep, dark wood showed its age gracefully, unlike the rest of the district. A layer of rust, grime, and oil coated everything down here. The door had only two of those things, and the oil seemed to enhance the wood's shine.

With a dull thud, the door shut behind Byron. The buzz of conversation fogged the air. Clinking glasses and sliding chairs created the perfect cacophony. He limped inside, weaving around a few people before scouting an empty stool at the far end of the bar. A broad-shouldered miner blocked the seat, but Byron slid into it anyway and squared his shoulders to earn his space. The man next to him grunted, but shifted to accommodate.

Byron spotted a flicker of blonde behind the kegs on the bar. He raised his hand to say hi, but Ms. Killian, the brewmistress, was too busy to notice him. Whatever. She'd get to him eventually.

In the meantime, he glanced at the nearby patrons' drinks. Pale yellow stuff. The head foamed on top of the drink like scum on a stagnant pond.

That thin ale was cheap to produce and easy to water down, which was why the brewmistress sold so much of it.

Most of the patrons coming into Killian's Taphouse just wanted a cold drink. This ale was certainly a drink and it was sometimes cold, so it did the job.

Byron appreciated the art and unique tastes in the brewing process. One of these days, he was going to brew his own beer and implement his own ideas. Flavors he'd heard about from bakeries with sweet breads and desserts, back from when he lived with his parents. He didn't have a taste for those things then—but now he was curious what cocoa and vanilla would do when incorporated into a malt, and how the hops would brighten the flavors.

The nearby miner clanged his tin mug on the counter.

"GERTIE!" shouted the worker. "FILL 'ER UP!"

Byron snickered as he heard Ms. Killian loudly huff behind the bar. She heaved a keg over her shoulder. Her curly hair was restrained in a ponytail at the back of her head, but the curls still fanned out in every direction.

"Excuse me?" she said, showing her teeth as either smile or sneer. This was a test—the worker had a chance to redeem himself.

"Gertie!" he repeated, less of a shout now that she was in sight. "I need a refill."

"Look, buddy, the name's Gertrude and nothing else," she snapped. She turned her attention to another patron, moving gracefully even with a full keg over her shoulder. Byron could hear the brew inside sloshing before she slammed the barrel down. After his day in the mines, his back cramped at the thought of heaving one himself.

Ms. Killian filled three tin cups simultaneously off of two taps. In a fluid motion, she spun around and slid all three shoddy brews down the counter. Each metal cup stopped perfectly in front of three patrons. Exchanging impressed nods, they took to their drinks and went on with their conversation. Ms. Killian beamed.

She made bartending into a dance. A feat of strength and

balance backed by a winning smile and a creative mind. The piss brew may have been her best seller, but it sponsored her more interesting beers.

Byron tried to picture himself running the taphouse with as much competency as Ms. Killian did, but he only imagined himself failing. One stumble on his bad leg would send him headlong into a tap, spraying sour beer onto the recurring sores on his cheeks. Nah. He'd be stuck in the mines until they swallowed him up.

"TRUDY! YOU HAVE A PAYING CUSTOMER OVER HERE!" The worker slammed his mug on the counter again. Grumbling, he turned to one of his buddies. "What ever happened to that 'squeaky wheel gets the grease' thing?"

His friend, a man of similar build, shrugged and buried his mustache into his cup for a long swig.

"Why waste grease? Broken wheels go in the trash," Byron muttered. He felt the worker's eyes on him.

"You wanna say that to my face, kid?"

"Trash," Byron said, turning slowly to the man, "belongs outside."

The man rose and threw a punch. Byron dodged backwards, falling off his stool. His back smarted when it hit the chipped vinyl floor. Mugs clanged and whoops rose from the patrons. The worker readied to plant a foot in Byron's stomach but froze as the bar went silent.

"OUT!" Ms. Killian stood on the counter, wielding a barstool like a club. "OUT BEFORE I CRACK YOUR HEAD OPEN!"

The brewmistress was a tower of a woman. She had several inches of height over this fellow—even before she stood on the bar—and had a muscular build from working to back up her threat.

Lowering his foot to the floor, the worker opened his mouth to spit something foul to her but decided against it.

He threw his empty mug behind the bar and trudged to the exit. Ms. Killian descended from her perch. Silence settled until the door thudded shut, when conversation sprouted up once more.

The mustached worker set his mug down before offering a hand to help Byron to his feet. Brushing himself off, Byron braced himself between his chair and the bar.

Ms. Killian set down a filled cup in front of him. A reddish brown liquid swirled inside, and the carbonation coalesced into a creamy, white foam on top.

"I was wondering where you were," she said as Byron settled in his seat.

"Amber?" asked Byron, sniffing. A sweet, wheaty smell.

"Pumpkin, actually," said Ms. Killian, retreating to the taps to fill the mustached man's cup. He gave her a polite nod.

"Ew. What's squash doing in a beer?" said Byron with a sour face.

"I dunno, what's a kid doing in my bar?"

"The same thing I've been doing since I was fourteen, you old hag," said Byron good heartedly. He tentatively took a sip of the stuff. Tart and a little too sweet. Needed more malt. "Daydreaming."

"Getting spoiled," said Ms. Killian. "You'll be brewing before long. Promise."

Terry Hojnacki

Terry Hojnacki, author of *I Can See With My Eyes Shut Tight*, is an award-winning flash fiction writer, children's book author, poet, novelist, editor, and lover of words. She is the founder and editor-in-chief of *Sterling Script: A Local Author Collection,* which is one of the many ways she works to promote her writing community.

Terry is a member of Detroit Working Writers, Society of Children's Book Writers and Illustrators, Rochester Writers, Sterling Heights Library Board of Trustees, and founder of Tuesday Morning Writers. She is the Creative Writers Workshop facilitator at the Sterling Heights Public Library, where she was named 2018 Volunteer of the Year.

Her short stories and poetry have appeared in *ARTIFEX, Ghostlight: The Magazine of Terror, Pink Panther Magazine, Nicole's Recurring Nightmares,* and *Sterling Script: A Local Author Collection.*

www.TerryHojnacki.com.

Night Horrors

Terry Hojnacki

"Mom, really you don't have to come. I just needed to talk for a few minutes, really. Kinda to regroup, ya know?"

The baby's cries echoed from the nursery. Each gaspy scream provoked another contraction. The colicky infant tortured the traumatized insides of its new mom.

"Honey, if you need me, I can be there tomorrow," Mary's mom said.

"No, no, really. I'll call you if I need to, really, I'll be fine."

"Honey, how's Annie?"

"Mom, I told you we're not going to be calling her Annie. Her name is Anna. If you want to shorten it, you can call her Ann, but we are not calling her Annie!"

"Okay, dear. How is Anna? You've rubbed her tummy like I suggested?"

"Fine. She's fine, Ma. I gotta go. I'll talk to you later." Mary cut off her mom's *I love you* as she ended the call.

There were advantages to having Mom living a couple time zones away. It was still early enough there to call and vent even though it was the middle of the night here. Anna lay in her cozy bassinet, screaming that high pitched "...uwa, uwa, uwa..." that only a newborn can scream.

Mary covered her ears to deafen the sounds of the wailing infant. She approached the baby's bed and looked in to see the innocent thing wiggling and crying in uncontrollable anguish. Gently, Mary tucked her hands under Anna's back and lifted the helpless infant.

Hoping the child would calm down, Mary cradled her. Back and forth, Mary's body swayed. Back and forth, Mary walked softly in the night. Anna cried and cried and cried. Mary rocked her back and forth.

Night after night, Mary was up with her colicky daughter. The pediatrician had said it was only a matter of time till she outgrew this. "Be patient," he'd said. Easy for a doctor to advise that approach when he wasn't the one up all night caring for the child.

Walking from window to door and back in the tiny nursery, Anna breathing heavily, but beginning to settle, Mary hummed. The song comforted her baby while it helped to comfort her as well.

After hours of nurturing, Anna slipped into a precious sleep. With slow, measured movements Mary settled her baby in the cradle and backed stealthily away from the bassinet. Like a spy having achieved their goal and just wanting to escape successfully, Mary turned the door handle, so, when it closed, she could turn it back without so much as a touch of the mechanism against the frame. Anna slept.

Mary leaned against the wall facing the nursery and stared at the closed door. A wave of exhaustion took over, and her body began to slip down the cool, smooth plaster. Catching herself, she tiptoed to her own sanctuary.

She slid under the warm blanket and snuggled next to her husband. He snored a monotone, white noise kind of snore. The darkness and the slow, melodious tone calmed her. Mary slept.

Then it happened! The roar! The shutter! The shake! An almost indescribable sound pierced the stillness. Her teeth clenched with six hundred pounds of pressure. Her jaw clamped, sending pain shooting through her head, her neck, and her back. She could feel the pain in her eyes as she tried to grasp what had just happened. Though not cold, she trembled. The shaking would not stop. The sound was worse than any fingernail on a blackboard, louder than an owl screeching as it swoops in on its prey. It bore into her temples and penetrated her brain.

The train had derailed in her bedroom. The engine still roared. It had to stop. She pushed and prodded her husband trying to get him to move. He was in such a sound sleep, no matter what she did his snoring continued. She pulled his pillow out from under his head. His snoring paused. He reached for a second pillow, tucked it under his head, and immediately snored again.

When the snore volume quieted to that of a loud television, Mary tried to go back to sleep. She wrapped her squishy pillow around her head to insulate her ears.

Then it happened again. It rumbled. It reverberated. It was no longer a melodic snore. It was a jackhammer. It was that damn train, followed by a racing motorcycle, and a car with a blown muffler! It was a rocket blast.

Mary hugged her pillow. She sobbed. She grit her teeth.

"It has to stop! It's going to wake my baby!"

With the rage of a volcano and the force of Mother Nature's anger, she slammed her pillow over his face and pushed as hard as she could. She was not going to let that snore start again. It would wake Anna. She couldn't listen to it anymore! Anna had to sleep. She smothered that snore with her pillow. She pressed harder and harder. The pillow tried to push back. Arms flailed. Legs kicked. With the strength of a mother bear protecting her cub, she held the pillow tight to the bed for as long. As. She. Could.

The noise had to stop.

No more snoring!

Finally, it was quiet. So quiet.

Mary collapsed and slept.

Last Breath

Terry Hojnacki

I held your hand the night you died
but I don't remember your last breath
I waited for it
watched for it
prayed for it

but your body, kept holding on
lungs inhaled air, shallow
heart beat, slow
blood pulsed through
veins in sagging skin
on brittle bones

my mind prepared for an end
to suffering, yours
and mine, knowing
there would never be
another love, only peace
and emptiness

when your time stopped
I missed it, and
in that surreal moment,
the tears didn't come
I held your hand the night you died
though I don't remember your last breath

Best Friend

Terry Hojnacki

a best friend is always there
supportive, kind, and brutally honest

they defend your mistakes
    then tell you how to fix them
they brag about your accomplishments
    then push you to do more
they feel your frustration,
    then force you to move on
they tell you the truth
    even when it hurts
they love all of you
    no matter what

your best friend is always there
you are your best friend.

Previous editions of
Sterling Script: A Local Author Collection
released in 2018, 2019, 2020, 2021

are available on Amazon.com
and through localauthorcollection@gmail.com.

ABOUT

Sterling Script: A Local Author Collection

Like us on Facebook at
https://www.facebook.com/LocalAuthorCollection

Would you like your flash fiction, short stories, poetry, art,
or creative nonfiction considered for publication
in our next volume?
Email **localauthorcollection@gmail.com**
to be placed on our mailing list.

Submission dates and guidelines for the
2023 edition of Sterling Script
COMING SOON

Made in the USA
Columbia, SC
26 November 2022